W9-AHA-920

DATE DUE

ALSO BY CLAUDIA MILLS

Makeovers by Marcia

MAKEOVERS BY MARCIA

Claudia Mills

FARRAR, STRAUS AND GIROUX
NEW YORK

www.fsgkidsbooks.com

Library of Congress Cataloging-in-Publication Data
Mills, Claudia.
Makeovers by Marcia / Claudia Mills.— 1st ed.
    p.   cm.
Summary: At the beginning of eighth grade, all Marcia can think about
is what nail polish to use, how to lose weight, and whether Alex will ask
her to the dance, but after giving makeovers in a nursing home for a
school project, she begins to pay less attention to outward appearances
and concentrate more on inner beauty.
    ISBN-13: 978-0-374-34654-6
    ISBN-10: 0-374-34654-2
    [1. Interpersonal relations—Fiction.   2. Old age—Fiction.   3. Nursing
homes—Fiction.   4. Student service—Fiction.   5. Schools—Fiction.]
I. Title.

PZ7.M69363Mak 2005
[Fic]—dc22

                                                          2004053248

To Joyce Richter

MAKEOVERS BY MARCIA

one

The scale had to be wrong. Marcia Faitak stepped off, then stepped back on again with her eyes squinched shut. When she forced herself to open them and look down, the red numbers on the digital display read: 110. At five foot three, she weighed one hundred and ten pounds. If the scale wasn't broken, this was the single worst thing that had happened to her in her whole entire thirteen and a half years of life.

The towel! The towel wrapped around her head had to weigh at least a pound, damp as it was from drying her shoulder-length dark hair. Marcia dropped it on the bathroom floor and checked the scale again. *Still* 110. A person couldn't weigh the same with *and* without a heavy, wet towel on her head. Could she?

Marcia bounced slightly on her toes: 112, 109, 111—then 110 again. She had weighed 105 in May, before her accident on the trail at seventh-grade outdoor ed. Now, after six weeks of lying on a chaise longue with a cast on her ankle, followed by a family vacation on a cruise where all they did was eat, apparently she had gained five pounds.

She remembered a joke Alex Ryan liked to tell. "Do you want to get rid of ten pounds of ugly fat? Cut off your head!" It didn't seem funny now. How could she start eighth grade tomorrow five pounds heavier, and with *two* newly erupted pimples, one on her forehead and one on her chin? The most important thing about eighth grade was that boys asked girls to go with them to the dances. In seventh grade, you just showed up with your friends and danced with whoever was there. What boy would ask a fat, pimply girl to go to a dance with him? Not Alex Ryan.

Back in her room, Marcia put on a pair of shorts—they *were* snug around the waist—and a bright blue, sleeveless, cropped T-shirt. She studied herself in the full-length mirror on her closet door. There was a visible bulge between the bottom of her T-shirt and the top of her shorts. She ripped off the cropped T-shirt and pulled on an extra-large T she sometimes used as a nightshirt. It hung down below her shorts, looking like a frumpy, baggy dress. Better that than let the world see the terrible truth about her protruding tummy.

Marcia picked up the phone and dialed her best friend, Sarah Kessel. Marcia knew that Sarah was monitoring two pimples of her own, lest they spoil her entrance on the first day of school.

Sarah started right in. "What are you wearing tomorrow?"

Suddenly Marcia wasn't sure she wanted to tell Sarah

what the scale had said. "I don't know. What about you?"

"My white shorts, the new ones I got last week? And my yellow top, with the daisies on the straps. I heard there's going to be a new dress code this year that says you can't have bare shoulders. Is that dumb, or what? So I figure I better wear my sleeveless tops while I can. Your blue top always looks cool on you—the cropped one?"

It was the shirt Marcia had discarded on the floor. Should she tell Sarah or not? "I don't know. I think it makes my stomach look too fat."

There was a silence on the other end of the line. Did Sarah agree that the blue top made Marcia's stomach look too fat, but not want to say it? Sarah certainly wasn't rushing to contradict her.

Marcia plunged ahead. "I weighed myself."

"Bad?"

"Very bad."

"How bad?"

"Very bad." She didn't know if she could say the number out loud.

"One-oh-eight?"

"Worse." Marcia was sorry she had mentioned her weight to Sarah in the first place, but now that she had, she might as well cut short the guessing game. "One-ten."

"You're kidding."

As if anyone would kid about something like that. Marcia refused to dignify Sarah's comment with a reply.

"You don't look that fat." *That* fat. "But I can see why you don't want to wear the blue top. You're sure your scale's not broken?"

"I weighed myself like a hundred times."

"Maybe you broke the scale, weighing yourself so much." Sarah laughed.

Marcia couldn't make herself laugh along.

When she hung up, she was more depressed after talking to Sarah than she had been before. Maybe she should call Lizzie. Lizzie and Marcia were opposites in almost every way, but Lizzie had been a good friend over the summer, when Marcia was recovering from her accident. Of course, brainy, nerdy Lizzie didn't like swimming, bike riding, or tennis, so it was hardly a sacrifice for her to sit out everything and keep Marcia company.

Lizzie didn't seem to think looks were important. That was the first way in which she and Marcia were opposites. Sometimes Lizzie dressed like everyone else, but sometimes she wore crazy clothes—such as long white dresses she had found in somebody's attic, which somehow suited Lizzie better than blue jeans. So Lizzie wouldn't think it was the end of the world if somebody gained a few pounds. But tiny Lizzie probably weighed seventy-five pounds, fully dressed. Marcia felt huge and hulking next to her.

The phone rang. Maybe it was Alex Ryan! Stranger things had happened. Marcia snatched it up.

It was her second-best friend, Jasmine Nolin.

"Sarah just told me," Jasmine said, her voice full of sympathy.

"Told you what?" If it was what Marcia thought it was, she was absolutely furious at Sarah. It had taken her all of two minutes to call Jasmine. Marcia could only imagine how long it would take Sarah to call the whole school.

"*You* know." Plainly Jasmine thought Marcia's new weight was too horrible to mention directly. "But I have a diet that really works. It's amazing."

Marcia didn't want to ask, but she couldn't help herself. "What kind of diet?"

"Grapefruit. Breakfast, lunch, and dinner. A whole one, with no sugar. Something about the acid in the grapefruit burns up fat, sort of eats it away or something."

How much fat could grapefruit eat away by eight-thirty tomorrow morning? Marcia didn't even know if they had any grapefruit in the house.

As soon as she hung up, she headed for the fridge. One slightly dented grapefruit was hidden in the back of the crisper. Marcia cut it in half and started eating. The sooner the acid could start its burning, the better. The intense sourness of the first bite made her mouth pucker.

"I don't believe it," her mother said, coming into the kitchen from the deck. "My daughter, the potato chip queen, eating a grapefruit?"

Marcia's mom had every platinum-dyed hair in place and wore carefully applied foundation, powder, blush, lipstick, mascara, and eye shadow, even for a day at home in the middle of the summer. She worked as a sales representative for a cosmetics company called Just the Way You Are, JWYA, or Jay-Dub for short. The Jay-Dub ladies sold Jay-Dub cosmetics at Jay-Dub parties at other ladies' houses. Marcia had lost track of how many Jay-Dub parties she had helped her mother with.

One good thing about the Jay-Dub connection was that Marcia's mother had let her wear makeup to school since she was in sixth grade. And she got tons of samples for free.

"I'm on a diet," Marcia explained. "Jasmine says grapefruit burns fat."

Her mother eyed Marcia's hidden waistline. "I told you those greasy potato chips have two hundred calories in one tiny bag. But I guess you had to learn it yourself, the hard way. I haven't eaten a potato chip in twenty years. You'd have to pry my jaws open with a crowbar and force one down my throat."

Marcia doubted anyone would want her mother to eat a potato chip that badly. But her mother was definitely slim, with all her curves in the right places. Sullenly Marcia swallowed another mouthful of the world's sourest grapefruit.

"Potato chips haven't done your skin any favors, either," her mother went on.

"I'm not eating them again. Can you buy me some more grapefruit? A lot more?"

"Diets aren't the way to lose weight, you know." At

least her mother got up and wrote *grapefruit* on the grocery list. "The way to lose weight is to eat a healthy, balanced diet and exercise aerobically three or four times a week."

That advice wasn't going to help Marcia lose any weight in the next twenty-four hours. Giving up, Marcia finished her grapefruit, put her bowl and spoon in the dishwasher, and then ran upstairs to reweigh herself.

111 pounds!

So much for help from Sarah, Jasmine, and Mom.

The only person Marcia had ever been able to turn to with her problems was her seventeen-year-old sister, Gwennie. Gwennie was really Marcia's half sister: they had the same father but different mothers. Gwennie lived half the time at Marcia's house and half the time with her own mom and stepdad. But Gwennie felt like a whole sister to Marcia.

Gwennie was at her other house today. Marcia pushed the button on the phone where she had programmed in Gwennie's number. Unfortunately, her mom answered. Marcia felt shy around Gwennie's mom.

"I'm afraid Gwen isn't here, Marcia. I expect her back any minute. Should I have her call you when she gets in?"

It was better than nothing. "Okay."

Clicking off the phone, Marcia looked at herself in the mirror again. She hadn't seen Alex for almost a month now; first his family had been on vacation, then hers. What would he say when he saw her at school tomorrow?

Alex was a great one for the clever insult, though when she had seen him at the pool off and on this summer, Marcia had noticed that he was less sarcastic than usual. Just as cute, though, with his broad shoulders and quick smile. "Hey, tub o' lard," she imagined him saying. "What crane hoisted *you* in here?"

She felt like crying. "Hormones," her mother said lately, whenever Marcia burst into tears about anything. "Women!" her father said, with a fond, superior smile. Well, they'd cry, too, if they weighed 111 pounds and had two pimples.

Hoping Gwennie would call back soon, Marcia kept the line free instead of checking her e-mail for the tenth time that day. Alex had e-mailed her when he got back from his family trip to the Grand Tetons. Marcia knew he felt guilty for having caused her accident at outdoor ed: he had hidden in the bushes and made a horrid rattling noise exactly like the sound of a rattlesnake ready to attack somebody. Terrified, Marcia had run down the trail, tripped, and broken her ankle.

But still, he didn't *have* to e-mail her that way. "I'm back. Just wanted to say hi. See you in jail. Alex." That sounded pretty friendly to Marcia.

She had e-mailed him back right away. "Hi to you, too. Did you see any rattlesnakes on your trip? What classes are you taking this year? Marcia." He hadn't written again. Maybe she shouldn't have said anything about rattlesnakes? But what good was guilt in a boy if a girl couldn't make use of it? She glanced at her watch. She could check her e-mail one more time, quickly.

The phone rang. Someone else on Sarah's calling list, with another diet suggestion?

"Marsh! What's up?" It was Gwennie.

"I'm fat!" Marcia wailed into the phone.

Gwennie laughed. "No you're not."

"Yes I am. I weighed myself. One hundred eleven pounds!"

"Well, you haven't been able to get any exercise this summer, with that awful cast. You'll lose it when you start doing P. E. again this fall."

"But school starts tomorrow! And my shorts are too tight. And my stomach pooches out. And I have two pimples."

"*All* your shorts are too tight?"

"The pair I have on now is."

"Okay."

Gwennie's voice took on the crisp, authoritative, problem-solving tone that Marcia was waiting for. Gwennie wouldn't tell her to eat grapefruit three times a day, either.

"Thing number one: Try on all your shorts and find at least one pair that fits. If you can't find any, I'll come get you and drive you to the mall. But you know Mom doesn't like me to do stuff with you guys on one of *her* days."

Okay, Marcia would try on shorts as soon as she and Gwennie got off the phone.

"Thing number two: Don't hide in some huge, baggy T-shirt. It'll make you look even fatter."

Marcia looked down at the nightshirt flapping around her knees.

"Thing number three: Cover the pimples with that Jay-Dub Vanishing Act cream. It works like a charm. But you knew that. Thing number four—are you still there?"

"I'm still here." Marcia loved Gwennie more than anyone in the world.

"Polish your fingernails *and* your toenails. Something outrageous. Tangerine is good. Purple Pizzazz is better. If they're looking at your nails, they're not looking at your tumkin. Got it?"

"Uh-huh. Oh, another thing? Alex Ryan? He didn't e-mail me back."

"Boys don't. It takes too much out of them. They have to conserve their feeble male strength."

"I told Sarah what I weighed, and two minutes later she told Jasmine."

"Not bad for Sarah. Have you ever known her to keep a secret that long? Listen, I gotta go."

"Thanks, Gwennie."

"Purple Pizzazz!" Then Gwennie hung up.

An hour later, Marcia had twenty pulsatingly purple nails. Maybe she was ready for eighth grade, after all— even if she was fat, pimply, betrayed by her so-called best friend, and ignored by the boy she had been flirting with for the past two years.

She inspected her nails again. The polish on her left pinkie had smudged. She opened her bottle of nail polish remover and prepared to do it over again. Her nails were all she had going for her right now. They had better be perfect.

two

Marcia weighed 110 in the morning. It was definitely better than 111, but still pretty sickening. She put on one of her three pairs of shorts that fit and a purple top to match her nail polish. Her hair looked somewhat better than usual, soft and dark and silky. Alex sometimes teased her with a quick pull on her hair. Maybe he'd do that today. He still hadn't e-mailed her back, though. Marcia had checked her e-mail twice already this morning. Nothing.

"Don't you look pretty," her father said when she presented herself in the kitchen.

"Oh, Daddy." He always thought she looked pretty, so Marcia could never take his compliments seriously. Still, he was sweet to say it.

"What do you want for breakfast?" her mother asked. "You left yourself all of five minutes to eat."

"Nothing. I'm not hungry."

"Is this that diet? *Especially* if you want to lose weight, breakfast is the most important meal of the day. I got you some grapefruit. I can scramble you an egg and fix you some toast to go with it."

Marcia's stomach rebelled at the thought of unsweetened, mouth-puckering grapefruit first thing in the morning. Still, yesterday's grapefruit had burned off one pound so far. "I'll have some grapefruit. No eggs or toast."

She made herself eat a few bites, until she could feel the acid start to take effect. "I'm full. Can we go?"

"Not so fast," her father said. "Eighth grade! Next year, high school! I need a picture of my baby." Marcia saw that he had his camera ready on the kitchen counter. He had taken a picture of her on the first day of school every year so far. All were framed and hanging on the wall in his office.

Marcia posed outside, in front of the same pine tree where she had stood for all her pictures. She remembered to suck in her stomach before the camera clicked. She'd have to work on holding it in all day.

Her mother drove her the mile to school. "Good luck, honey. You *do* look nice."

Her mother's compliments were more rare and meaningful than her dad's. "Thanks."

Marcia hopped out of the car and looked around for Sarah, Jasmine, or Lizzie. First she found Sarah, easy to spot in her bright yellow daisy top. "I'm mad at you," Marcia said by way of greeting.

"Why?"

Marcia didn't answer.

"Because I told Jasmine and Keeley and Brianna that you'd gained some weight? We're your *friends*. We want to *help* you. Did you try the grapefruit diet? Jasmine says it's like a miracle how fast it works."

Marcia couldn't stay mad at Sarah for long. She would have done the same thing if Sarah had said something like that to her. She was surprised that Sarah had stopped after telling three other people.

"Oh, and I guess I told Brittany and Lizzie. But Lizzie doesn't really count, and Brittany—did you know her sister has a weight problem, too?"

Too.

"And she lost *fifteen* pounds this summer. You can ask Brittany how she did it. I think she used that diet where you eat bacon all day long."

"Bacon? Nothing's more fattening than bacon."

"All I know is that she lost fifteen pounds doing it. I think the fat in the bacon acts like a magnet for the fat in your body. Sort of fat attracts fat."

As she was half listening to Sarah, Marcia scanned the gathering crowd for a glimpse of Alex. She saw his best friend, Dave Barnett, and short Ethan Winfield, who was always paired with tall, gangly Julius Zimmerman. And Travis Edwards, Sarah's current crush, tall and good-looking, but not as tall and good-looking as Alex. But there was no sign of Alex anywhere.

Then someone grabbed her from behind, covering her eyes with his hands.

"Guess who?" a falsetto voice asked.

Marcia's heart soared. "Let go of me, Alex Ryan!" She

broke free from his "blindfold" and whirled around to face him. He grinned at her. She smiled back.

Sarah had tactfully withdrawn as soon as Alex appeared. It occurred to Marcia to hope that Alex hadn't overheard the tail end of their conversation. "Fat attracts fat" was not the image a girl wanted to burn into a boy's brain.

"Where's your schedule?" Alex asked.

Marcia shrugged off her backpack as gracefully as she could and pulled her schedule from her pink binder.

"Hand it over," Alex said.

Marcia waited for his report. *Please, oh please, let us have lots of classes together.*

"We're in math and French together, and social studies and English. Are you ready for the Cow again?"

Marcia giggled. She and Alex had taken a summer French class together a year ago and suffered through strict Madame Cowper. Marcia had thought about switching to Spanish, which was supposed to be easier anyway, but her father said it would be foolish to waste the French she had already learned, so she'd be in Madame Cowper's company for second period all year. At least Alex would be there with her.

"It's Williams who's supposed to be the real killer," Alex said, still studying Marcia's schedule. "Social studies. She thinks we should all go out and save the world. You're taking art? I didn't know you were into art."

Apparently Alex had never seen Marcia's sketches of

him in her math notebook. "I like to draw." She should have taken art last year instead of chorus.

"Let's see how much you like it after Morrison is through with you."

"Is he mean?"

"My sister, Cara, had him. I don't know if you'd call him mean, exactly, but— Well, you'll see."

The bell rang. The sixth graders started running. The seventh graders started walking. The eighth graders stayed in their small groups talking.

"Shall we?" Alex asked. They sauntered into West Creek Middle School together.

First period was math with ancient, doddering Mr. Adams. He spoke in a whispery wheeze that could barely be heard and held on to the chalkboard ledge with his free hand while he wrote on the board with trembling, arthritic fingers. The class, even Alex, was surprisingly well behaved, as if afraid that at any moment he might keel over right in front of them.

"I thought they made teachers retire before they're ninety-five," Alex said to Marcia as they walked down the hall to French.

Marcia giggled again.

Madame Cowper's broad face brightened when she saw them. "Mademoiselle Faitak, Monsieur Ryan, *entrez, s'il vous plaît!* Come in! *Je suis enchantée de vous revoir.* I am so happy to see you again!"

Marcia greatly doubted this was true. Alex in particular

had been awful throughout Intensive Summer Language Learning two summers ago, and she herself had laughed appreciatively at all his antics, as well as at his jokes about Madame Cowper's stout figure stuffed into snug polyester pantsuits. It would take more than Purple Pizzazz nail polish to deflect the eye from Madame Cowper's plump posterior. But given the events of the last twenty-four hours, jokes about someone's weight didn't seem as funny to Marcia anymore.

By the end of class, Marcia decided that French would be pretty easy, given her head start from the summer class. She remembered quite a bit, even from a year ago. Her father had been right, after all.

Ms. Williams, the third-period social studies teacher, was extremely tall and elegantly slim, in a bright red suit with a crisp white blouse that set off her dark skin. Her erect posture reminded Marcia to suck in her own stomach.

In eighth-grade social studies they would cover civics and debate important, controversial issues of the day, Ms. Williams said. Marcia snuck a sidelong glance at Alex. Would it be more romantic to be debate partners or debate opponents? She didn't know.

"My approach to teaching," Ms. Williams went on, "is centered on service learning. Does anyone know what service learning is?"

No one did, not even Lizzie.

"In service learning," Ms. Williams explained, "students learn through community service. Each of you will engage in one major service project of your own choosing. I expect you to devote three hours a week to it. Of course, this will be in addition to time spent on outside reading, paper writing, and studying for exams."

That was a lot of time to devote to any one subject. Already protesting hands were in the air.

"I'm on a traveling soccer team," one boy said. "We go on the road practically every single weekend. I'm not going to have time to do three hours a week of community service."

"I don't design the requirements of my course to accommodate your extracurricular activities. I expect you to arrange your extracurricular activities to accommodate the requirements of my course."

"But—what if you just can't do it?" the boy asked.

Ms. Williams gave an elaborate shrug of indifference. It was clear that the shrug meant: *Then you fail.*

Alex's friend Dave asked the next question. "My mom's a single mother. She's too busy to drive me anyplace."

"I have prepared a list of possible service opportunities, many of which are within easy bicycling distance of school."

"What if you don't have a bike?"

Marcia knew that Dave was baiting Ms. Williams now. Dave had a bike. Everyone did, except for Lizzie Archer.

"My experience has been that the vast majority of students have bicycles. If you do not, special arrangements can be made."

Another student raised her hand. "Do we have to do one of the things on your list, or can we think up something on our own?"

Marcia tried to think of possible community service projects that she and Sarah could stand doing. Make a Web site to answer the twenty most frequently asked questions about clothes and makeup? Organize a dating service for socially challenged eighth-grade girls? The dating service would be a good idea, now that Marcia thought about it. She might need it herself if she couldn't get Alex to ask her to the first eighth-grade dance. The dance was the second weekend in October. A lot of girls were going to be getting nervous by the middle of September.

Marcia waited to see what Ms. Williams would say.

"I am open to your ideas," Ms. Williams said, "but any service project you undertake for this course will have to be approved by me."

So much for the fashion Web site and the dating service.

"What if we don't like any of the things on your list, and you don't like any of the things on ours?" That was Alex.

"Then I will choose a project for you."

Marcia envisioned herself assigned something truly horrible, such as picking up litter by the roadside. Or cleaning outhouses in one of the nearby mountain parks. Or helping to feed drooling, senile old people in a nursing home. She and Sarah would have to think of something cool enough to do but noble enough to appeal to Ms. Williams.

Ms. Williams's steely expression softened. "From many years of experience, I predict that 90 percent of you will tell me come May that service learning in this class was the most meaningful and satisfying part of your eighth-grade year."

Marcia had a feeling that she would be among the 10 percent who wouldn't. She certainly hoped so. She hated to think how pathetic her eighth-grade year would be if community service was the best thing in it. She imagined writing in Sarah's yearbook at graduation, "Remember the great time we had in the nursing home?" And Sarah writing in hers, "Wheelchairs forever!"

Fourth period was P.E.; fifth period was lunch; sixth period was English, with exotic Ms. Singpurwalla, whom Marcia had had for English last year. The seventh-period science teacher, Mr. Dorr, told lots of lame jokes. Marcia made a feeble effort to giggle appreciatively.

Marcia was glad she had art eighth period. The best should be saved for last, like dessert after a long, dull meal—not that Marcia should even be thinking about dessert these days.

Mr. Morrison looked like an art teacher, fairly young,

bearded, dressed in worn black jeans and a black T-shirt. "Take out your sketch pads," he told the class.

Two kids had forgotten theirs, though "9 × 12 spiral-bound sketch pad" was on the school supply list that had been mailed home over the summer. Mr. Morrison didn't say anything to those students. He simply acted as if they weren't there.

"Draw something," he said.

Marcia opened her brand-new box of colored pencils and selected a pink one. She'd draw a beautiful girl with huge blue eyes and long, swirling blond hair who didn't need to lose five pounds to fit into her favorite shorts.

She started drawing. The picture turned out pretty well. Sometimes Marcia's girls had one eye bigger than the other, or closer to the nose, but this time both eyes were perfect. Marcia added some dark, fringed eyelashes. The only problem with being blond in real life was having light brows and lashes.

"Who's that?" Mr. Morrison asked, looking down over Marcia's shoulder.

What did he mean, who was that? Were they supposed to make up a story to go with their pictures? Marcia wasn't good at making up stories. She wasn't a writer, like Lizzie.

"Just a girl." Marcia knew it was the wrong answer as soon as she said it.

He frowned. "Barbie." When Marcia didn't reply, he

went on: "You've drawn Barbie. Same hair, same eyes, same impossible figure."

Marcia gathered from his tone that drawing Barbie was bad. Millions of people around the world loved Barbie. Apparently, Mr. Morrison was not one of them.

"In my class, students do not draw Barbie."

Marcia didn't ask him why not. She didn't want to antagonize a teacher on the first day of school and have him pick on her for the rest of the year.

"What should I draw?" She kept her voice appropriately meek.

He exploded. "Anything!" Well, anything except Barbie. "Draw what you *see*. Draw the pencil sharpener. Draw the faucet on the sink. Draw the back of the head of the boy in front of you. I'm not going to tell you what to draw!"

He stomped off to glare at somebody else's picture. Marcia tore "Barbie" from her sketch pad and stared at the next blank sheet of paper. She looked at the back of the head of the boy in front of her. There was a pimple on his neck, not covered up by any Jay-Dub vanishing cream.

Between cleaning outhouses for Ms. Williams and drawing pimply necks for Mr. Morrison, eighth grade was going to be terrific.

three

Marcia and Gwennie were both helping at a Jay-Dub party that weekend. Marcia had to help. Gwennie didn't, but she had a great relationship with Marcia's mother.

"Besides," Gwennie told Marcia as they were getting into the car, "I can write about the Jay-Dubs on my college application essays. The admissions people are always looking for something different, and I'm sure no one else will be writing 'My Life as a Junior Jay-Dub Lady.' "

The party was held at a huge house, all windows looking out over a swimming pool and a private tennis court. The lady hosting the party, who claimed that her name was Muffin, showed them into the stunning family room, with a massive stone fireplace and soaring skylights.

"We'll have the party in here," Muffin said.

Marcia looked for outlets to plug in their three large makeup mirrors, each one framed with bulbs chosen to give the most flattering possible light. Gwennie draped a navy blue tablecloth over the card table they had lugged in and began laying out the various makeup samples.

"You haven't told me anything about school yet," Gwennie said, as soon as Marcia's mother had bustled off to the kitchen to confer with Muffin about the party plans.

"Alex is in four classes. He made a big thing about comparing our schedules on the first day. And he did send me an e-mail last night."

"Saying?"

" 'Wasn't I right about Williams?' " Five words, but at least it was something.

"Who's Williams?"

"The social studies teacher. She's going to make us all do service learning. You know, performing good deeds in the community. You have to help me think of something Sarah and I can do that won't be too disgusting."

"This shade is new." Gwennie held up a bottle of brownish-pink nail polish. "Ashes of Roses. I like the name, but I'm not sure I like *it*. I don't see the point to nail polish unless it makes people sit up and take notice. What kind of good deeds do they have to be? I don't suppose assisting at a Jay-Dub party would count."

"You work with the same group all year, like Save the Whales, or a church or something, or maybe you could tutor poor kids after school—I don't know. I don't want to get something gross, like picking up dog poop on trails or changing old people's diapers at a nursing home."

Marcia turned on the first mirror and peered at her reflection. It was a hot afternoon, and her face looked flushed and sweaty from hauling the makeup mirrors in from the car. But the two pimples she had been so worried about had almost disappeared.

"Tutoring could be fun," Gwennie said. "Little kids always love their teachers."

"Maybe." Marcia wasn't one of those girls who adored being followed around by little kids. Julius would probably sign up for tutoring. Over the summer Marcia had seen him dragging some noisy little boy to the pool in a red wagon.

"We had a career-planning workshop last year at school," Gwennie said, "and they said to find the thing that you love to do most in the world and try to make a career out of that. Maybe that would work for your service learning, too. Start with whatever you love to do, and see if you can use it to do a good deed for someone else."

Marcia thought for a moment. What *did* she love to do? Experiment with makeup. Talk on the phone to her friends. E-mail Alex. Draw—well, she *had* liked drawing until Mr. Morrison had come along and ruined it for her with his Barbie crack on Thursday.

"What do *you* love to do most in the world?" Marcia asked Gwennie.

"Anything to do with people," Gwennie said unhesitatingly. "Watching them, talking to them, trying to figure them out. What about you?"

"I don't know." Even to Gwennie, Marcia wasn't about to say aloud the only things she had thought of so far.

"*I* do. You like looking good, and hanging out on the phone with your friends, and flirting with boys, and anything to do with art." The look on Marcia's face must have given her away because Gwennie laughed. "Am I right? So now you know where you need to look to find some good deeds to do."

Marcia laughed, too, but then she said, "There are no good deeds that involve flirting with boys."

"How about: Makeovers by Marcia. Free fashion advice for the aesthetically challenged."

"Well, Ms. Williams has to approve our projects, and I don't think she's going to let us do that kind of thing."

"You don't know till you try."

Marcia's mother came back into the room with Muffin. Marcia would have expected a person named Muffin to be small and round, but this Muffin was as tall and elegant as Ms. Williams. If Marcia's own name had been Muffin, or Doughnut, or Danish Pastry, she would have changed it.

"Everything looks very nice, girls," Marcia's mother said. "Muffin, I would have given up the Jay-Dub business long ago if it weren't for these two."

"And wouldn't you know that they don't need a speck of makeup, either one, not like us old gals."

Marcia caught Muffin stealing a glance at herself in one of the makeup mirrors. She could tell that Muffin liked what she saw.

"Muffin, you don't look a day over thirty, and you know it," Marcia's mother told her.

"And *you* don't look a day over twenty-eight. But I have to admit I'm not above seeking some help. I'm planning to have Dr. Phillips do my eyes this fall. That'll hold me for a few years, until it's face-lift time."

"Phillips is good. He did Lacy Jones's eyes last year, and, I tell you, the *difference*. He took ten years off that woman's face."

"You're lucky you haven't needed yours done yet."

"Soon." Marcia's mother sighed. "I'm such a coward about surgery, I hate to admit it. But I know I'm reaching the limit of what Jay-Dub products can do for me."

Marcia wished they would stop talking about operations. The thought of a surgeon's knife cutting away at someone's face made her feel sick. She had seen her mother's friend Lacy right after the operation, looking as if someone had beat her up in a dark alley. And as far as Marcia could tell, once the bruises faded, Lacy didn't look any better than she had before, despite all her mother's appreciative gushing.

Gwennie came to the rescue. "I don't suppose you need anyone to sample the refreshments, do you, Muffin?"

Muffin smiled indulgently. "They're all in the kitchen. Go help yourselves."

Muffin's second fridge was filled with tray after tray of

hors d'oeuvres. Marcia was starving, but she settled for one small cucumber sandwich. There were hardly any calories in a cucumber.

On Monday, Ms. Williams was wearing a tailored, crisp white linen dress, accented with a vibrant lilac-patterned scarf at her throat. Marcia had to give credit where credit was due: the woman knew how to dress.

"Today we'll make the service-learning assignments," Ms. Williams said. "I want you to be able to contact your sponsoring organization as soon as possible so you can begin logging your hours."

She switched on the overhead projector. A list of local service organizations appeared on the screen. Sure enough, certain predictable names were on the list.

Creek County Parks and Recreation. *Outhouses*, Marcia thought. *Dog poop*.

West Creek Manor Nursing Home. *Diapers*.

YMCA After-School Enrichment Program. *Snotty little noses*.

"What about our own ideas?" Alex asked. "Don't you want to hear them first?"

"All right," Ms. Williams said pleasantly. "What service projects have you come up with over the weekend?"

Marcia hesitantly raised her hand. Three other people had hands up, too: Alex, Dave, and Lizzie Archer.

"Lizzie," Ms. Williams said. Teachers always called on Lizzie first. It used to drive Marcia crazy, the way teachers fawned over Lizzie, but Marcia was used to it by now. Lizzie couldn't help being a great big brain in a tiny little body. That was who she was. And Lizzie had been smart enough to come to Marcia for advice on clothes and boys.

"I was thinking," Lizzie said in her high, breathless voice, "that there are so many old people in West Creek, who have lived so many years and have so many stories to tell, and one of these days they'll die, and if we don't listen to their stories, and write them down, they'll be lost forever. So my project would be to talk to as many older people as I can and preserve everything they tell me. I thought I'd call the project 'Saving the Stories.' "

Leave it to Lizzie to earn Ms. Williams's first real smile of the year.

"That is a wonderful idea, Lizzie. There's a growing movement to gather oral histories before it's too late. I'll put you down as a volunteer at West Creek Manor Nursing Home. I know the residents will be thrilled to have you take an interest in their memories. All right, Dave, what did you have in mind?"

"Alex and I— Well, we thought— We could watch— Maybe this isn't a great idea, but—" He wilted under Ms. Williams's expectant gaze.

Alex took over. "We think there's an important need for a team to conduct research into the content of after-school television programming for children, to watch all of the cartoons that are being broadcast on various networks and monitor the amount of violence on each one, and the amount of advertising as well."

Marcia waited to see what Ms. Williams would say. Surely she couldn't fail to notice that Alex and Dave's project involved nothing more than watching hours of dumb cartoons every day, supposedly in the name of scholarship.

"And the *service* dimension of your project would be? Remember, these are not intended to be *research* projects but *service* projects."

"We think our report itself would be an important community service," Alex said. "We could present it at a press conference, and maybe even get some local TV coverage of our findings."

"No," Ms. Williams said. It was clear that her "no" was final. "In service learning, students work with sponsoring organizations to provide community service, not on their own to conduct independent research, however valuable."

If "however valuable" was intended as sarcasm, Ms. Williams hid it well.

"Marcia, what is your idea?"

Marcia couldn't go through with it, not after hearing Ms. Williams shoot down Alex's proposal. "Never mind."

"I'd like to hear it," Ms. Williams said.

Why wouldn't she let it drop? All right, Marcia would just say it and be done with it, and if everybody laughed, she'd laugh, too, as if she had meant to be funny all along.

"I thought I'd do, well, makeovers, for people who really need them."

"Makeovers?"

"Like in the magazines. Before and after? Fix up their hair, and see what colors look good on them, and try on different kinds of makeup, and do their nails."

Ms. Williams looked thoughtful, as if she was actually considering Marcia's idea. "And your sponsoring organization would be?"

"I don't have one," Marcia admitted.

Ms. Williams tapped the overhead with her marker. "I'll put you at West Creek Manor Nursing Home with Lizzie. I can't think of any people who would be more appreciative of what you're offering."

Before Marcia could protest, the deed was done. There was her name, written underneath Lizzie's, to spend a whole entire year volunteering at the very place she had dreaded most. She turned and met Sarah's eyes, wide with horror, then looked away. She couldn't bear the thought that Sarah would pity her. *Poor Marcia, first she gained all that weight, and then Ms. Williams signed her up for the nursing home.*

Ms. Williams continued signing kids up for projects. Sarah chose after-school tutoring, with Julius. Marcia started to wish her dozens of runny noses, but then stopped. It wasn't Sarah's fault that Marcia had gotten assigned to the nursing home. Sarah pitied her from friendship, not from spite.

Dave got assigned to Community Food Share. Ethan looked pleased at getting maintenance work on the mountain trails. One by one, each kid raised a hand to choose a project and was entered on Ms. Williams's master list.

Except for Alex.

"You still haven't chosen anything," Ms. Williams said to him.

"There's nothing here I want to do."

"Should I pick something for you, then?"

He shrugged.

Ms. Williams studied the list. "I only have two names so far for the nursing home. Why don't I put you there, with Lizzie and Marcia?"

"To do what?"

"I'm sure the staff can find some kind of appropriate project for you. What talents do you think you can bring to this project?"

Alex didn't answer. Marcia knew he wasn't about to say: a sarcastic sense of humor, clever practical jokes, excellent toilet-papering of people's trees. He had T.P.ed her tree last year, and she still had a scrap of toilet paper saved in her treasure box.

"I'm sure you'll think of something," Ms. Williams told him. "They have a big Oktoberfest party there every year. Maybe you can help with that."

Marcia hoped Alex would look pleased that they were assigned to the same place, but he refused to smile. Still, their names looked nice, side by side on the overhead.

If only they hadn't been written side by side next to "West Creek Manor Nursing Home."

four

Marcia made herself call West Creek Manor Nursing Home that day after school. She was hoping the lady who answered the phone would say, "Oh, service learning? We don't do that program anymore. It was too disruptive for our residents to have all those young people traipsing through." But the lady didn't. At least she said that Marcia didn't have to begin her service hours until the following week. And first there would be a mandatory "orientation" for all the students from all of Ms. Williams's eighth-grade classes who would be helping that year. At the orientation, they'd watch a film and have refreshments.

The lady said "have refreshments" as if she expected Marcia to be overcome with joy at the very thought of a plateful of store-bought sandwich cookies and a paper cup of punch. Marcia just thanked her politely and hung up. They would have to pry her jaws open with a crowbar to force punch and cookies down Marcia's throat. She still weighed 109 after five solid days of dieting.

"You've hit a plateau," Gwennie told her over the phone. "All dieters hit one sooner or later. You don't eat, and yet you don't lose weight. It's the greatest frustration of dieting."

Well, that and not being able to eat any of your favorite foods, such as potato chips and sour cream onion dip, and mint chocolate chip ice cream drowned in chocolate sauce.

"But it's impossible," Marcia protested. "If you eat fewer calories, you *have* to lose weight. It's like a law of physics. Didn't Isaac Newton say something like that? 'A body in motion will remain in motion.' 'A body that doesn't eat will lose weight.' I'm almost sure he did."

For the first time, Marcia wished she had paid more attention in one of her classes at school. Who would have thought that something as boring as her last year's science class would be so directly related to Marcia's own life?

"The problem is that your metabolism changes," Gwennie explained. "You eat less, and that sends a signal to your body to burn calories more efficiently, so you eat less and you *don't* lose weight."

"That," Marcia said, "is the single most unfair thing I have ever heard of in my entire life." She had been pacing back and forth across her room with the cordless phone. Now she threw herself down onto her bed. It sounded like something a man would dream up. Isaac Fig Newton probably hadn't had to worry about *his* weight. Alex ate three times as much as Marcia, she could tell from spying on him in the school cafeteria, and he was solidly muscled, with not an ounce of extra fat.

"So what do I do?" Marcia asked. "Kill myself now?"

"You exercise. That tells your metabolism that you need to burn up more calories, and you do, and then you can eat even more than you did before and still lose weight."

Marcia considered this. She wasn't the athletic type. She didn't like sports where you had to hustle and sweat. For a few years in elementary school she had been on a soccer team, but by the final year the whole thing had gotten too competitive for her. She remembered one girl on the team, Ashley. It had been the biggest thing in Ashley's life whether or not her team scored a goal. Marcia preferred sports like tennis, where you could wear flouncy little skirts to show off your long tan legs. If you had long tan legs. After her summer of convalescence, Marcia had chubby white legs.

"Like what kind of exercise?"

"Any kind. Walking. Walking is great. Wait. I have a brilliant idea. Are you going to be there for another ten minutes?"

"Sure."

"I'll be right over."

After Gwennie hung up, Marcia stayed on the bed, studying the shape of her stomach under her shorts and T-shirt. It was satisfyingly flat when she was lying down. From her nightstand she grabbed her sketch pad. Mr. Morrison had said to keep it handy at all times in case they saw something beautiful or interesting that they wanted to capture. He should have said to keep it handy so they wouldn't die of boredom while lying in bed trying to keep their stomachs flat.

She drew another "Barbie," to spite Mr. Morrison, but she gave her a bigger nose than any real Barbie would ever have, and a noticeable stomach bulge. Let Barbie see what it was like not to be perfect! Let Barbie see what it was like to have the big dance inching ever closer and no invitation yet from Ken. Of course, it was only the second week of school, and Marcia knew that no boy was even thinking of asking a girl to the dance yet. It would take some serious, but subtle, manipulating by the girls to plant the seed of that thought in the dry, stony soil of an eighth-grade boy's brain.

"Hey."

Marcia looked up to find Gwennie standing next to her. She had been completely lost in her silly drawing.

"Close your eyes," Gwennie said.

Marcia obeyed. Gwennie put something into her hand, small and hard, a palm-sized case made of smooth plastic. "Okay, open."

Marcia opened her eyes. The thing in her hand looked exactly the way it felt—like a palm-sized case made of smooth plastic.

"It's a pedometer. My mother sent away for it once when she was on an exercise kick, but her kicks never last long, so she gave it to me."

"What's it for?"

"It counts every single step you take. You can program it so that it converts steps into miles. But it's more fun just counting the steps."

Gwennie took the pedometer, clipped it onto her belt, strode several times around Marcia's room, then clicked it open to check the count. "Thirty-seven steps."

"Let me try it." Marcia pushed the reset button, clipped on the pedometer, and walked the same circuit Gwennie had walked, counting each step to herself. "Thirty-five steps." She checked the pedometer. It said: 41.

"So it's not completely accurate," Gwennie said. "It's close enough. Your goal is ten thousand steps a day."

"A *day*?" Marcia yelped. "Ten *thousand*? You've got to be kidding."

"They add up fast. Walk to school instead of letting Dad drive you. Help with yard work. Walk over to Sarah's house instead of calling her on the phone. You'll get to ten thousand in no time."

Marcia made a face. Gwennie laughed. "Calculus is calling me." Gwennie continued counting steps out loud as she walked out of Marcia's room: "Thirty-eight, thirty-nine, forty . . ."

As Gwennie's car pulled out of the driveway, Marcia laced up her sneakers. She couldn't get to ten thousand steps today, starting so late in the day, but she could get to three thousand maybe. That would be three thousand more than nothing.

Once outside, she thought about where to go. She wasn't in the mood for Sarah. Sarah's favorite topic these days was Marcia's weight and whether or not it had changed in the past hour—and how sure she was that Travis Edwards was going to ask her to the October dance.

Marcia turned her footsteps in the opposite direction from Sarah's house, fully aware that the road stretching off that way led right past Alex's cul-de-sac.

She walked briskly, not that the pedometer knew or cared how rapidly she accumulated her total number of steps. Although she was dying to check it after every block, she vowed not to peek until the entire walk was over.

He probably wouldn't be there anyway. He was on the middle-school track team, so he was most likely off running. No wonder he could eat as he did and not gain weight.

Maybe she'd bump into him while he was finishing up his run. But then he'd be with the rest of the team and wouldn't be able to do more than grunt to acknowledge her presence. Marcia practiced the small smile she would give in response to the grunt. It had to convey pleasure at the sight of him, but some measure of superior amusement, too. *Boys! Ridiculous creatures! But this particular one is undeniably quite cute.* That was a lot to put into one small smile. But Marcia knew she was equal to the task.

Then, all at once, there he was, coming up from behind her, not running with the team, but all alone on his bike.

"What are you smirking about?" he asked, braking neatly to a full stop by her side.

There were few things more embarrassing than being caught practicing the perfect smile. Marcia felt herself blushing. "Nothing."

He accepted her answer. "Where are you off to?"

Marcia felt her blush deepen. "Nowhere. I'm just out for a walk."

"Ankle doing okay?" Alex sounded uncomfortable now.

Marcia remembered something she had read in an advice book on dating. It said the woman should always make the man feel masculine, by stressing how big and strong he was, even if she was trying to tease or insult him. If you had a fight—and some playful little spats kept a relationship interesting—you should make sure you called him such names as "big brute" and "hairy beast."

"Well," Marcia said, striving for a lighthearted tone, "it would be doing better if some big brute hadn't practically attacked me on the trail."

Was that too much? "Big brute" sounded pretty absurd when it was actually said out loud to someone, rather than printed on a page in a book.

Alex winced. "Aw, Marcia . . ."

One "big brute" remark per conversation was probably enough. "It's basically fine. I can play tennis, and dance, and everything." She took pains not to emphasize the word "dance." But it seemed to hang in the air between them.

Speaking of dancing, the eighth-grade dance in October? You don't want to go with me, do you? If only Alex would say it.

"Did you call the nursing home yet?" he asked.

Oh, well. The dance was still almost six weeks away. Marcia nodded. "We don't have to start until next week. After this orientation. We have to watch a movie. And have refreshments."

Alex's face brightened. Marcia would let him eat her share of cookies. The way to a boy's heart was through his stomach, right? She tried to think of something else to say so he wouldn't pedal away.

"Well, see you at school tomorrow," Alex said.

Marcia gave him a smile, intended to say: *I want to go to the dance with you, you hairy beast, so hurry up and ask me, because if someone else asks me first I'll go with him instead.* But he was gone before she had a chance to complete the message.

No longer in the mood for a walk, Marcia turned around and headed home. She checked the pedometer the minute she was inside the house: 1,385 steps. Plus one halfway-significant conversation.

Shortly after art class began the next day, Mr. Morrison strolled around the room, glancing through students' sketchbooks, looking over their shoulders at the water-color still lifes they were attempting. In the front of the room he had set a single red apple, positioned on a white plate. It wasn't exactly the most inspirational thing Marcia had ever been asked to draw.

"*Still* doesn't mean *dead*," Marcia heard him say to one student. "That apple isn't made out of plastic. It's a real piece of fruit that I picked myself yesterday from a real tree."

Marcia greatly doubted that. Mr. Morrison didn't look like the apple-picking type. On her own paper, she dutifully painted a round thing and colored it a nice bright red. There. One apple.

"You," Mr. Morrison said to her. "What's your name?"

"Marcia. Marcia Faitak."

"All right, Marcia Faitak. Name three ways in which an apple is different from a red-colored tennis ball."

What was she supposed to say to that? When she didn't answer, he said, "One, an apple is not perfectly round. Two, an apple was not mass-produced in a factory. Three, you can eat an apple."

Did he think he was being funny? Or did he just like to hear himself talk in his bored, sarcastic way? Marcia would have come up with a different list. An apple is sweet, juicy, and delicious. An apple has eighty calories. An apple is one of the few snacks a dieter is allowed to have.

"See if you can draw something edible," Mr. Morrison said. Then he was off to the next student's desk.

Well, Marcia had to admit that her apple *did* bear a striking resemblance to a red-colored tennis ball. If it was even that interesting. It was more of a red-colored round thing.

All right. If Mr. Morrison wanted her to draw something edible, she'd draw something edible. Marcia stared at the juicy, red, mouth-watering apple glistening on the white ceramic plate on Mr. Morrison's table, and dipped her brush back into her paint. But what she really wanted to do was snatch the apple off the plate and take one great big bite out of it.

five

The orientation at West Creek Manor was held the following Tuesday at 7 p.m. Marcia had thought about e-mailing Alex to see if he wanted a ride, but it seemed too much like chasing him—probably because Marcia's reason for doing it *was* to chase him. Instead she rode to the nursing home with Lizzie.

Lizzie's mother drove them. Mrs. Archer was different from the other West Creek moms. An English professor at the university, she had long hair like a college student's, only now turning gray. All her clothes were about twenty years out of style, if they had been in style then. She wore no makeup at all. Marcia was sure that Lizzie's mother had never attended a Jay-Dub party and never would.

"Good evening, Marcia," Mrs. Archer said when Marcia slipped into the back seat next to Lizzie. "How's eighth grade so far?"

That was the standard question all the parents asked.

"Okay, I guess."

"What have you been reading lately for fun?"

That was the kind of question that could only have come from Lizzie's mother.

Marcia strained to remember the title of the last book she had read. She couldn't come up with anything. "I mostly read magazines. *Seventeen. Glamour. Cosmo.*"

Had Mrs. Archer cringed? What would she have done if Marcia had told the truth, that she mostly read catalogs?

An awkward silence descended on the car. Marcia wished Lizzie's mother would give up, but she knew Mrs. Archer would make another strained attempt at conversation. Sure enough, she asked one last question. "What clubs will you be in at school this fall?"

Lizzie was the star of the math team and the new editor of the literary magazine, and she played flute solos all the time in the orchestra. Marcia and Sarah had always thought it was dorky to get involved in dumb school clubs. If the middle school had had a cheerleading squad, Marcia might have tried out for it. "Give me an *A*! Give me an *L*! Give me an *E*! Give me an *X*! What does it spell? *ALEX*!" But cheerleading didn't start until high school.

"I'm not into *clubs*, exactly." Marcia had to think of something else to say. She couldn't bear to have Lizzie's mother thinking she was a complete and total zero. "I help my mom in her business sometimes. And—um—I've been walking a lot. And I've been doing some drawing."

"I didn't know you liked art," Lizzie said.

Was it going to turn out that Lizzie was also an accomplished artist who had her work on display in the Denver Art Museum? Was there anything Lizzie Archer couldn't do? Actually, Marcia knew that Lizzie wasn't good at sports. And until last year she hadn't had very many—any?—friends. Marcia still remembered how mean she herself used to be to Lizzie, back in sixth grade.

"It's not like I'm good at art, or anything," Marcia said uncomfortably. "I just like drawing things."

"Do you want to give me something for *Creek Dreams*?" Lizzie asked. "We publish art, too, you know."

"Maybe." Marcia couldn't imagine submitting one of her drawings to Lizzie. What if Lizzie said it wasn't any good? It was bad enough being sneered at by Mr. Morrison; it would be intolerable to be rejected by Lizzie Archer. Besides, no one Marcia knew read *Creek Dreams*, except for the parents of the nerdy kids who had stuff in it.

"You girls are in for some interesting experiences at the Manor," Mrs. Archer said then.

Interesting? It wasn't the word Marcia would have used.

"I know," Lizzie said. "I'm a little bit scared. I hope—Well, I hope it won't be too sad . . . these people in wheelchairs, who were once so active, living out in the world, who had families and friends, and now have nobody to visit them. All they have is their memories. If they still have their memories. That would be the worst thing—to have hardly any future, and such a dreary present, and then to lose your past, too."

Lizzie was starting to sound distraught. She was always

the emotional one, who cried real tears over some sad book in English class that Marcia hadn't bothered to finish. But Marcia felt uneasy about the nursing home, too. It was bound to be depressing to see all those old people sitting there.

"At least they'll have you two to visit them now," Lizzie's mother said.

When they reached the nursing home, Mrs. Archer dropped the girls off at the front entrance and drove away. Marcia and Lizzie looked at each other.

"I'm scared, too," Marcia admitted.

Inside the lobby, a pleasant-looking, not-old woman greeted them. "Are you girls here for the orientation? It's in the dining room. Straight down this hall, and then turn left."

The nursing home was attractively decorated. On the freshly painted pale green walls were pictures of cheerful landscapes showing gardens overgrown with roses in full bloom and sailboats drifting on sunny seas. It had a funny smell, though, a harsh odor of antiseptic mixed with . . . Marcia hoped the other smell wasn't old people's pee.

The hallway was vacant, except for a sad-eyed lady standing silent in her doorway and two old men parked in their wheelchairs near the nurses' station. Marcia felt shy as she approached them. Should she say hi, or not?

"Pretty," one old man croaked to them. Marcia forced a smile. "See you later, darlin's," he said, and winked. Marcia fought the urge to turn and run back out to the parking lot. There were worse things in life than failing social studies.

"He's just being friendly." Lizzie sounded as if she was trying to convince herself as much as Marcia.

"I know," Marcia said.

Everything felt different once they reached the dining room. A dozen West Creek eighth graders were already talking and laughing by the refreshment table. Marcia checked: Alex wasn't there yet.

"Do you want some punch?" Lizzie asked, holding the ladle over an empty paper cup.

"No thanks," Marcia said. "I'm on a diet."

"*You're* on a *diet?*" Lizzie almost shrieked. "You don't weigh anything!"

"I bet I weigh thirty pounds more than you do," Marcia shot back. It was easy for Lizzie to say that Marcia didn't need to lose weight.

"I'm practically a midget," Lizzie said lightly. "Everyone in the world weighs more than I do. But you—you're perfect. You're beautiful. You don't need to lose a single *ounce.*"

"Well, I'm not hungry or thirsty right now," Marcia said.

"I'm hungry *and* thirsty."

It was Alex. Lately he was always materializing out of nowhere at inconvenient moments. Marcia hoped he hadn't heard their conversation about dieting.

Alex crammed a couple of cookies in his mouth,

washed them down with a long gulp of punch, then said, "Did you see those geezers in the hall? One of them whistled at a girl walking ahead of me. I think they're looking for dates."

"Maybe one of them will go with me to the eighth-grade dance," Marcia said. Instantly she was sorry she had said it. It made her sound pathetic—the Girl Without a Date. It was true that nobody had a date for the dance yet. But this sounded as if she didn't expect ever to have one. Also, it sounded as if she was fishing for Alex to ask her, right then and there, to save her from going to the dance with geezers. Not that he could ask her in front of Lizzie.

"You'd better brush up on your Charleston," Alex said.

Marcia refused to laugh.

"West Creek students!" a tall woman with a beehive hairdo called out. Marcia had never seen a person with a beehive hairdo in real life before. The staff at the nursing home might need makeovers, too. Marcia's fingers itched to wash the hair spray out of the woman's teased-up hair and let it fall naturally around her face. She'd have to do something about her eyebrows, too. The natural brows were gone—plucked out? The painted-on ones were shaped to give the woman's face a look of perpetual surprise. She wasn't that old, either; she could be passable-looking with a little help.

"Please find a seat, and I'll run the video," the lady said.

Marcia, Lizzie, and Alex sat down at the closest table.

Alex took the seat next to Marcia, rather than the one next to Lizzie. That was something.

The beehive lady turned on the large-screen TV and switched off the lights. The video began. It made West Creek Manor sound like the best nursing home in America. The grounds looked like an extensive park, though Marcia hadn't been all that impressed when Mrs. Archer drove in. The hallway that Marcia and Lizzie had walked down looked longer and more spacious, and no leering old men loitered there. The residents shown were busily engaged in craft projects, singing at a party they called the Oktoberfest, boarding buses in their wheelchairs for excursions to the mountains. Everyone was smiling.

When the video was over, the beehive lady switched the lights back on and began explaining the rules for student volunteers. All volunteers had to sign in and sign out and wear an official VOLUNTEER badge. They were to be given a list of residents to visit for that day and were to enter only the rooms designated on their list. Many of the residents were on special diets, so no food gifts were to be given to anyone without permission. Appropriate behavior toward the residents was to be observed at all times. Anyone failing to follow any of these rules would not be allowed to continue as a West Creek Manor volunteer.

"Boohoo," Alex fake-sobbed to Marcia.

"Any questions?" the lady asked. "Oh, Ms. Williams told me one of you wants to interview the residents for an oral history project. That's wonderful, but do ask permission before tape-recording or photographing anybody. And one of you wants to do—I believe it was beauty makeovers for our residents?"

Someone laughed. Marcia sank lower in her seat to make herself as small and inconspicuous as possible.

"That's fine, too, but do make sure you don't upset the residents in any way. You might want to check with the staff about the particular preferences of individual residents before you offer your services."

Or you might want not to offer your services at all.

"Any questions?" the beehive lady asked again.

Nobody had any, not even Alex, though under his breath he whispered to Marcia, "Like, hey, lady, what happened to your hair?" He made a low buzzing sound, in apparent imitation of a swarm of bees heading home for the night.

"If there are no more questions, well, then, thank you for your kindness in volunteering to help us this year. We'll see you back here next week."

Marcia didn't feel all that kind. None of them wanted to be there, not even Lizzie. They were there because Ms. Williams was making them come in order to pass eighth-grade social studies.

"My mom's probably here by now," Marcia told Lizzie. "It's five past eight, and I told her I thought we'd be done by eight o'clock."

The girls started back down the hallway, ahead of the

others, who had stopped to grab one last cookie. The old men were gone, thank goodness. But the sad-eyed lady was still standing in her doorway. Had she been standing there the whole time?

"Girls," she called to them softly.

Marcia and Lizzie stopped walking.

"Do you have a minute? I have some special things I want to show you."

Marcia was glad that Lizzie answered for both of them. "We can't right now. But we're coming back soon, to visit lots of people. I hope we can visit you then."

"It will only take a minute."

The beehive lady had told them the rule: don't enter any rooms except those designated on the day's list. And Marcia's mother probably *was* waiting. And if there was anything in the world Marcia didn't want to do, it was see whatever the lady had to show them.

Then, in a small voice, Lizzie said, "Okay."

"Lizzie . . ." Marcia hissed at her warningly. But when Lizzie entered the room, Marcia had no choice but to follow.

The floor of the room was bare linoleum, and the bed was a hospital-type bed with an ugly metal frame, but the quilt was bright and colorful, and every wall was covered with framed family photos.

"This is my son, Robbie," the woman said, pointing to a picture of a young man in a military uniform. "Here he is as a baby." The picture showed a chubby toddler with a sticky face and a big smile.

"Where does he live now?" Lizzie asked.

"He was killed in Vietnam," the lady said. "October eighteenth, nineteen sixty-seven. That was the day he died. 'Friendly fire,' they called it. Shot by mistake by his own side."

"I'm sorry," Lizzie whispered. Marcia tugged at Lizzie's sleeve. She didn't think she could stand being there another minute.

The beehive lady appeared in the doorway. "Mabel, these girls need to go home now."

"We'll be back to see you again," Lizzie promised faintly. Marcia hoped Lizzie was wrong.

A tear rolled down the woman's cheeks. "I still miss Robbie every day."

"Come, girls," the beehive lady said gently.

Out in the hall, Marcia waited to see if they were going to be fired as West Creek Manor volunteers, given that they had broken one of the most important rules on the very first day. *Please fire us, please fire us, please, please, please!*

"We knew we weren't supposed to go into the residents' rooms," Lizzie said. "But she looked so sad. And she said it would just take a minute."

Marcia saw Lizzie's eyes fill up with tears.

"I know," the beehive lady said, putting one arm

around Lizzie and the other around Marcia. "There's a story in every one of these rooms that can break your heart if you let it. Good night, girls. West Creek Manor is lucky to have both of you."

It was lucky to have Lizzie, maybe. But if Marcia had her way, she'd drive away from West Creek Manor that night, and never ever come back.

six

Two days later, Sarah and Marcia were standing beside their lockers after school when Travis Edwards stopped by.

"Hi, Sarah," he said. And then he stood there, grinning like—well, "like an idiot" was the expression that came to Marcia's mind.

"I was wondering . . ." he said.

"Wondering what?" Sarah asked with the coy little smile she had learned from Marcia.

Then one of Travis's friends came along and yanked him away.

"Wondering what?" Sarah almost shrieked to Marcia after Travis was out of earshot. "Do you think he was wondering what I think he was wondering?"

"Well, I don't think he was wondering if you'd done the math homework yet," Marcia said, trying to look happy for her friend. But if Travis asked Sarah to the dance and Alex didn't ask Marcia . . . It couldn't happen. Marcia simply couldn't bear for it to happen.

The next day, Travis stopped Marcia in the hall when she was on her way to math; he wasn't in any of her classes. "Hey. Marcia. How's it going?"

"Okay," Marcia said. She didn't think Travis wanted details about her weight, her first visit to the nursing home, or her relationship with Alex.

"I was wondering—" Travis began, and then broke off.

More wondering? There was the same shyness in Travis's eyes that had been there when he had stopped at Sarah's locker yesterday. Was he now going to ask *her*, *Marcia*, to the dance?

Instantly Marcia was on the alert. She would never deliberately take a boy away from any of her friends, but if the boy came crawling up to her, of his own free will . . . Still, it was Alex she wanted to go to the dance with, Alex and no one else. But she wasn't going to wait forever for him to ask her, either.

"Yes?" Marcia knew her large blue eyes were her best feature. She opened them wide and glanced up at Travis through long, dark lashes.

"The eighth-grade dance?"

"Yes?" She let her lips curve into an encouraging smile. Travis really was very cute. His light brown hair, a little too long, hung down over his eyes.

"Do you think . . . ?"

Travis stopped again. Marcia tried to hold her smile, but she was beginning to feel the way she did when her dad called out "Say cheese!" and then fiddled with his camera for another five minutes.

"If I asked . . ."

Come on!

"Do you think Sarah would go with me?"

Marcia could feel her face crumpling into visible disappointment. Quickly she slapped a new smile into place: the knowing smile of a wise, secure, more experienced, but still extremely attractive older woman, giving advice to foolish young lovers.

Now Marcia had to think of what to say. Sarah certainly did want to go to the dance with Travis, every bit as much as Marcia wanted to go with Alex. Sarah wanted to go to the dance with Travis more than anything in the world. But Marcia couldn't say *that*.

"I think . . ." Marcia said slowly, as if considering the question for the first time. "Yeah, I have a feeling . . . I mean, if you asked her the right way."

"Would you do it? Ask her for me?" He grinned at her confidentially.

So Marcia, who had no date for the dance yet, was supposed to bustle about arranging Sarah's date for her?

"I think she'd be more likely to go if you asked her yourself." She tried to keep the impatience out of her voice.

"I will. But could you just sort of . . . ask her if she *would* go with me if I *did* ask her?"

"Okay." She forced herself to give the secret smile of one conspirator to another.

"Great. You're going with Alex?"

Marcia squirmed. What was she supposed to say to

that? A lie was too dangerous; the truth was too humiliating. "Who knows."

"You girls." Travis shook his head in obvious despair and admiration.

The bell rang. Marcia was officially late for math. Old, decrepit Mr. Adams always gave extra homework for tardiness.

Thanks a lot, Travis Edwards.

Marcia sat in French class later that morning, trying not to think about her weight *or* the dance. It was hard.

Marcia had seen T-shirts that said, "So Many Books, So Little Time," intended for people like Lizzie and her mother. Marcia's T-shirt would have to say, "So Many Grapefruits, So Little Weight Loss." She had been taking every extra step she could, as measured by her pedometer, and she had lost one more pound. But one pound wasn't enough. One pound was nothing.

Maybe the acid in the grapefruit stopped working after a certain point. Or maybe she shouldn't have eaten that whole entire large bag of potato chips last night, after she had decided she couldn't live another minute without the wonderful salty crunchiness of potato chips in her mouth. Her mother never bought potato chips, but Marcia knew her father had a brand-new bag inside the little cupboard in his home office.

He didn't have one anymore.

"Quel temps fait-il aujourd'hui?" Madame Cowper was asking somebody.

Marcia knew that meant: What is the weather today? She gazed outside the classroom window. It was sunny, as it was almost every day in Colorado.

"Il fait beau," the kid replied. It is beautiful.

It *was* beautiful. The tree outside the classroom window was starting to turn from green to gold. The lawn underneath was littered with the first fallen leaves, stray patches of pure yellow. Marcia felt like drawing them in her sketchbook. But she didn't have her colored pencils with her.

The leaves on the ground made her think of the tree outside her window at home. Its leaves were starting to turn, too. *And* her father had made a deal with Alex last spring that this fall he would come over to rake them, to make up for breaking a branch while he was toilet-papering it. Marcia remembered how happy she had been the next morning, to step outside and see the tree festooned with miles of toilet paper. She had known right away that it was Alex. She and Gwennie had had so much fun pulling the paper down and letting the long streamers trail behind them, like wisps of lace on a bridal veil.

Marcia glanced at Alex now, conveniently sitting right next to her. Did he remember his promise? Was he looking forward to having an excuse to come over to her house? Or was he dreading it? If a boy liked a girl enough to T.P. her tree, shouldn't he also like her enough to invite her to the eighth-grade dance? That seemed only logical. But sometimes Marcia thought that the male brain was totally devoid of logic.

"Mademoiselle Faitak." Madame Cowper spoke her name. *"Quel temps fait-il à New Delhi en Inde?"*

Marcia had to think for a minute. What is the weather in New Delhi, India? How would she know? For all she knew, or cared, India could be in the middle of a monsoon. *"Il fait chaud?"* she ventured. It is hot?

"Très bien." Very good.

Alex hadn't been called on yet. Marcia expected him to give some funny wrong answer to his weather question—that it was snowing in the Sahara Desert or boiling hot on the summit of Mount Everest.

But the world's weather wasn't enough to distract Marcia from all her bleak thoughts. She didn't have the nerve to pull out her sketchbook, so she turned to a blank page in her French notebook. Ignoring the pale-blue, college-ruled lines, she started to draw Madame Cowper standing by the chalkboard. Madame Cowper was wearing one of her usual too-tight polyester pantsuits. She looked much better in the flowing caftans she wore on special occasions, and a caftan would have been easier to draw. But Marcia concentrated on drawing what was in front of her eyes, as Mr. Morrison had told her to. A real apple, not a red tennis ball; a real person, not a Barbie doll.

Marcia drew carefully: the teacher's enormous legs,

poured into the two bulging tubes of her pants; the teacher's buttoned jacket, with the buttonholes gaping and straining across her ample stomach; the way Madame Cowper's folds of chin hung down over her collar.

She could feel Alex's eyes on her, looking at the drawing in the notebook. Too late, she covered it with her forearm. Alex had already burst out laughing.

"Monsieur Ryan," Madame Cowper said. "*Pourquoi ris-tu?* Why are you laughing?"

Alex didn't answer; his shoulders were shaking from suppressed guffaws.

"*Est-ce qu'il y a quelque chose d'amusant?* Is there something amusing?"

"No," Alex managed to say.

"*En français, s'il te plaît.* In French, please."

"*Non.*"

Madame Cowper was approaching down the aisle. The desks were positioned closely enough together that her thighs brushed against them as she walked.

"Mademoiselle Faitak?" Madame Cowper's eyes fell on Marcia's notebook, still shielded by her arm. The teacher held out her hand. "*Donne-le moi.* Give it to me."

Marcia felt sick. But she was too paralyzed with horror to refuse. She handed Madame Cowper her notebook.

Madame Cowper stared down at Marcia's drawing. A dull red flush spread over the teacher's face and neck.

"I'm sorry," Marcia whispered. "I didn't mean . . ."

"You draw very well," Madame Cowper said quietly.

For the first time since school had begun, she spoke entirely in English. "This is an accurate likeness. I do not think, however, that there is much kindness in it."

She handed the notebook back to Marcia and returned to the front of the room.

She called on Alex as if nothing had happened. "Monsieur Ryan, *quel temps fait-il en été?*" What is the weather in summer?

"*Il fait chaud,*" Alex said. It is hot. It might have been the only time Marcia had ever heard Alex give an answer to a teacher's question without a wisecrack in it.

seven

Marcia waited until after school to tell Sarah about the conversation with Travis. She felt bad waiting, but there were too many other girls around at lunch, and Marcia couldn't face speculation from Jasmine, Keeley, Brianna, and Brittany on why Alex hadn't asked her yet. Plus, the memory of Madame Cowper's face when she saw the drawing still burned in Marcia's chest as if she had swallowed a live coal.

"Guess why I was late to math?" she quizzed Sarah as they headed outside for the 2,317-step walk home. "I'll give you a clue: somebody stopped me in the hall to ask me an important question."

"Alex!" Sarah squealed. "You're going to the dance with Alex! Why didn't you tell everybody at lunch?"

"No, it wasn't Alex." Marcia tried to keep the bitterness out of her voice. "It was—Travis!"

Marcia hadn't realized Sarah wouldn't understand. Of course, when Travis had made his first awkward mention of the dance that morning, Marcia hadn't understood, either. Sarah's face fell, and she turned away, clearly to hide her disappointment and wounded pride.

"To ask me if I thought *you* would go to the dance with him!" Marcia finished triumphantly, unable to let Sarah suffer a second longer.

Sarah whirled around, her face ablaze with happiness now. "For real? You're not making this up? What did you say?"

"I said I thought you *might* consider it, if he asked you the right way. I'm supposed to kind of test the waters, find out what you would say *if* he asked you."

Sarah flung herself into Marcia's arms. "You're the best friend in the whole wide world! I '*might* consider it.' How do you think of stuff like that to say, right on the spot?"

Marcia soaked up Sarah's praise. It was good to know she hadn't entirely lost her touch. "Practice."

"Okay," Sarah said importantly. "Tell him . . . What should I have you tell him?"

"I'll come up with something," Marcia said. "He needs to know you like him, that you like him a *lot*, but you're not *desperate* about it, and you'll go to the dance with him if he asks you, but he needs to ask you *soon*, or you'll go with someone else." All the same things someone needed to tell Alex about Marcia. "I can handle it."

Marcia suddenly remembered one dumb part from the Shakespeare play called *A Midsummer Night's Dream*, which they had read in English last year. There were these two lovers who lived on opposite sides of this wall, and one actor in the play was the Wall. That was his whole part, to make a little hole with his fingers so that the

66

lovers could use him to talk back and forth to each other. Right now Marcia felt like the Wall.

"But what about *you*?" Sarah asked then, as the girls started walking again.

Marcia almost wished Sarah hadn't remembered. She had planned to nurse her hurt feelings in silence a little bit longer. "Oh, don't mind me. I'll just stay home the night of the dance and do my nails."

"Marcia! We *have* to make Alex ask you!"

"Maybe I should get somebody else to ask me."

"Like?"

"Julius?"

Sarah looked thoughtful. Then she shook her head. "I've seen him with some girl who doesn't go to West Creek."

"Maybe it was his sister."

"This girl was not his sister. Julius doesn't have a sister, does he?"

"What about Dave?"

Sarah didn't make a face, but she didn't look thrilled with the suggestion, either. "I guess that would count as sending a message to Alex. But it's risky. If you really like Alex. You know how boys are. Once you hurt their pride."

"What about me? I have some pride, too."

"What *is* it with Alex? Why isn't he asking you?"

Marcia blinked back tears, glad they were walking fast enough that Sarah couldn't see her face. "I don't know."

Why *wasn't* Alex asking her? Of course, the dance was still a little over four weeks away; as of this morning, Travis hadn't asked Sarah yet, either. Marcia knew Alex liked her, or he wouldn't hang around her as much as he did, and he wouldn't have toilet-papered her tree last spring, though that was a long time ago now. Marcia hadn't told anyone, not even Gwennie, that she had saved a piece of toilet paper from the tree and had hidden it in the carved wooden box where she kept special things.

Sarah was right. If Marcia really liked Alex, she shouldn't flirt with his best friend.

And she really did like Alex.

If he didn't ask her to the dance, maybe she *would* stay home and do her nails. She looked down at them now. The Purple Pizzazz had been replaced with Wild Strawberry, which had been replaced with Electric Blue. Electric Blue, Marcia decided as she inspected her hand, was a truly hideous color for nail polish. On the night of the dance, if she wasn't going with Alex, she'd do her nails with Ashes of Roses and burn her cherished scrap of toilet paper, all alone up in her room.

If she wasn't going with Alex.

After school on Monday, as Marcia's mother drove them to their first official afternoon of service at West Creek Manor, Marcia and Lizzie didn't talk much in the car. Lizzie had a tape recorder and a camera, as well as her usual floral-covered notebook. Marcia had a tote bag full of Jay-Dub samples.

"When I thought up this oral history project," Lizzie finally said, "I forgot how bad I am at anything to do with machines. I know I'll press the wrong button at some point and wind up erasing the whole thing. And every time I try to take a picture of anybody, I cut off the top half of the person's head, or the whole picture is this huge blurry pink thing that turns out to be my thumb."

Marcia laughed. Lizzie wasn't exaggerating her mechanical ineptitude. In sixth grade Lizzie had been the only kid who couldn't light a bunsen burner; in seventh, she had caught her hair in a sewing machine in their family-living class.

The girls fell silent again. Marcia almost said, "Well, when I dreamed up this makeover project, I didn't know I'd have to be putting lipstick and eye shadow on people who are a hundred years old." The thought of touching someone that old gave her the creeps.

"Maybe we should play chess with them," Marcia suggested as her mother pulled into the long drive leading to the manor. "Like Alex is doing." She had heard him tell Ms. Williams that he was going to take his chessboard with him on his first visit to the nursing home, and Ms. Williams had said that was a great idea.

"I don't know how to play chess," Lizzie said.

"Neither do I."

Both girls laughed.

"Now, don't be nervous," Marcia's mother said. "I'm sure whatever you do will be greatly appreciated."

"Do you think that whatever *Alex* does will be greatly appreciated?" Marcia whispered to Lizzie. It was hard to imagine cutup Alex solemnly playing interminable games of chess with a bunch of doddering old people.

Both girls laughed again. Marcia felt a surge of friendship for Lizzie. Whenever you laughed together with someone, it made you feel a lot closer afterward. Maybe she should try to laugh with Alex—at something other than her sketch of Madame Cowper.

Once inside the nursing home, the girls stopped at the reception desk to sign in and get their volunteer badges.

"I have the list of residents for everyone to visit today," the receptionist told them. This was not the beehive lady, but she, too, could have used a makeover. Her dyed jet-black hair contrasted harshly with her tired, pale face, and Marcia could see a full inch of gray roots extending on either side of her part. If only Marcia could grab a black Magic Marker for a quick touch-up!

The lady squinted down at the list. "They've put you two together. I believe they're putting everybody in teams."

Marcia felt weak with relief. Lizzie looked relieved, too. Marcia wondered if she'd ever be paired with Alex, but right now she was glad to be partners with Lizzie. Being partners with Alex would have added a stress of its own, and Makeovers by Marcia was stressful enough already.

"Mrs. Mavis Getty," the lady told them. "Room one twenty-four."

The door to the room was open. The TV was on. A woman sat in a wheelchair, facing away from them.

"Mrs. Getty?" Marcia called from the doorway. The volume on the TV was so loud the woman couldn't hear.

"Just barge right in, girls!" one of the male aides said as he came up to them with an armful of clean linens. "She won't bite!"

The man strode past them into Mrs. Getty's room. "Mavis! There's two girlies here to see you." He turned the wheelchair around and clicked off the TV. "Now, isn't that nice? Not one visitor today, but two!"

Mrs. Getty smiled at them uncertainly. She was a large woman, almost as heavy as Madame Cowper, with bright red hair and crooked orange lipstick. "Which one of you is Diana?" she asked.

"I'm Lizzie," Lizzie said softly, "and this is Marcia."

"You'll have to speak up," Mrs. Getty said. "Who did you say you were?"

"Lizzie." Lizzie spoke loudly and clearly this time.

"Marcia." Marcia did the same.

"Where's Diana?" Mrs. Getty asked. "Isn't she here? Diana? My great-granddaughter? Jerry's girl?"

"I don't think so," Marcia said. "Does she go to West Creek Middle School?"

"She lives in California somewhere."

"I don't think she's here," Marcia said. "But *we're* here, Lizzie and me, and . . ." And what? And we think people with red hair shouldn't wear orange lipstick? And that particular shade of red hair is most often seen on circus clowns?

Lizzie took over. "I'm doing a school project where I interview people. About their childhoods, where they grew up, where they went to school, and what the world was like back then. Would you mind if I interviewed *you*?"

Mrs. Getty beamed. "Not at all! Sit right down, both of you. Over there, on my bed. Shove the newspapers out of the way. Your friend, the pretty one, is she going to interview me, too?"

Marcia knew she must be "the pretty one." If only Alex thought so, and not just Mrs. Getty. And if only her project weren't so hard to explain. "My mother works for a beauty product company, and I have some samples—of lipstick? And nail polish? And I thought it might be fun if—"

"A makeover!" Mrs. Getty chortled with glee. "For eighty-four years I've read those magazines every month, watching other gals getting makeovers and wondering when it would be my turn. And it's today?"

Marcia nodded, glad that Mrs. Getty looked so pleased.

"But now—you won't do anything to my hair, will

you? You're not going to hack it all off, are you? Those magazine makeover folks, seems the first thing they always do is chop off somebody's hair. A woman's hair is her glory, that's what I've always believed. And natural red hair is the most glorious of all."

Natural red hair?

Mrs. Getty laughed. "Well, it was natural once. And that's all that counts, right, girls?" She winked at Lizzie, who had red hair, too.

Marcia found herself liking Mrs. Getty. She was certainly more fun to be with than the sad-eyed woman they had met last time.

"All right, Diana," Mrs. Getty said to Marcia. "You don't mind if I call you Diana, do you? What part of me are you going to make over first?"

"Maybe . . . Well, why don't you take off the lipstick you have on." Marcia handed her a box of tissues. "And we'll try a different shade, one that complements your hair. And then we can do your nails in a matching shade. All our Jay-Dub lipsticks have nail polish to match."

"And you, Diana number two," Mrs. Getty said to Lizzie. "I can talk while she does her fixing and fussing. I talked through the Great Depression. I talked through a world war. About the only thing I ever shut up for was Elvis Presley. When he came on *The Ed Sullivan Show*, I didn't scream and carry on like those other gals, oh, no. I watched him, and I fell in love. Now, my husband, Frank, he couldn't sing a note, not one single solitary note, but he had Elvis Presley's eyes. I might've preferred Elvis Presley's hips, but I was lucky to get his eyes. It was a good marriage, all in all. I've been awful lonely since Frank passed away three years ago this October."

Marcia saw Lizzie scribbling away in her notebook, as fast as she could write. Mrs. Getty hadn't given her time to turn on the tape recorder. Marcia held up a dark red lipstick—Autumn Flame. It was several shades darker than Mrs. Getty's hair, but hair like hers needed toning down, not bringing out. She'd try some green eye shadow, too, a hint of it, to draw attention to Mrs. Getty's best feature, her wide green eyes.

" 'Love me tender,' " Mrs. Getty started to sing, crooning into an imaginary microphone.

"Wait." Lizzie pressed a button on the tape recorder.

Marcia checked; it was the right one.

Mrs. Getty started the song again as Marcia began rubbing Jay-Dub moisturizing cream into her cuticles. It didn't feel any stranger to be manicuring Mrs. Getty's nails than it did to do the nails of the ladies at Muffin's party. Her skin felt surprisingly soft and warm, not creepy at all.

When Marcia had finished the first hand, Mrs. Getty held it up for inspection. She crowed with delight.

"Have you girls met the new man in Room Two-nineteen? From Nashville, Tennessee? When he talks southern to me, it's like Elvis Presley whispering right into my ear. I might go waggle these nails at him when you gals are done with me."

As Mrs. Getty kept talking, Marcia started on the other hand, determined to give Mrs. Getty the manicure of her life. If the old man from Nashville didn't fall head over heels for Mrs. Getty, it wouldn't be for want of Marcia's trying.

eight

Marcia decided against making an elaborate speech to Travis. Boys didn't care about subtlety or nuance or exactly how much some girl liked them on a scale from 1 to 10, where 7.2 meant "She likes you a lot, but you'd better ask her to the dance quickly before somebody else does," and 7.4 meant "I think if someone else asked her, she might stall, hoping to hear from you." Instead, Marcia simply caught Travis's eye as she passed him in the hall on the way to French class. He raised an eyebrow; she smiled and gave him a thumbs-up. Simple and elegant.

If only Marcia could think of a simple and elegant way to let Madame Cowper know that she was really truly sorry about the picture she had drawn last week. Marcia was surprised by how sorry she was. Two summers ago, when she had taken Intensive Summer Language Learning, she had laughed louder than anybody else when Alex had called Madame Cowper "the Cow" and made comments about all the fattening French foods she probably shoveled in all day long. But gaining five pounds herself had made Marcia look at fat people in a new way. She wondered if Madame Cowper also weighed herself every day and hated the number she saw on the scale.

Marcia didn't say anything to Madame Cowper. It was hard to imagine what she could say. She tried to smile with special apologetic friendliness when Madame Cowper greeted the class. But she didn't think Madame Cowper even noticed.

In art class that day, they were drawing more still lifes. This time Mr. Morrison had brought in an apple that had seen better days. It was bruised and dented on one side, as if it had been too long forgotten at the bottom of the crisper. The good thing about drawing a picture of a half-rotten apple was that you couldn't hurt its feelings by making it look withered and shriveled and ugly. Marcia took special pains with her drawing. No one could say her apple looked like a tennis ball now.

"Good!"

Marcia froze. Was Mr. Morrison talking to her? She hadn't known the word "good" was in his vocabulary. She hadn't expected it to be used on any drawing of hers. But, sure enough, he tapped her paper approvingly with one ink-stained finger.

"You're coming along. You're looking at things now. That's what art is all about. Drawing and painting what you see in front of you."

Even your French teacher bulging out of her polyester pantsuit?

As he turned to go to the next student's desk, Marcia decided to take a chance: "What if you drew a picture of somebody, and—well, you made them look exactly like they do in real life, but the trouble is that they look—well, awful in real life?"

Mr. Morrison didn't answer right away. Maybe it had been a dumb question. Then he said, "You're not the first artist to ask this. It's every portraitist's dilemma, the duty to tell the truth versus the need to cater to vanity. Especially if you want to get paid. The great artists told the truth, most of them. That's why they're great. Wander through the galleries of any of the world's most famous museums, and you'll see portraits of some seriously ugly people."

He didn't understand.

"But what if—I mean, if you're not getting paid, or anything, and it's not that the person you're drawing is vain exactly, but that—you made her look ugly, and you hurt her feelings. No one wants to look *ugly*."

"Ahh." Mr. Morrison took another long pause. "The great artists painted ugly people in all their ugliness, but the other reason they're great artists is that they also painted people in all their beauty."

Now it was Marcia's turn not to understand.

"Come here."

Mr. Morrison led Marcia over to a low bookcase filled with art books. He pulled out one of the fattest books and opened it at random to a portrait of a stout woman with a starchy ruff around her neck.

"Do you know who this artist is?" he asked.

"Um, no." Marcia had always thought museums were boring. When Madame Cowper had taken them that summer to the Denver Art Museum to see the French Impressionists, all Marcia had cared about was how mad she was that Madame Cowper hadn't let Alex come on the trip, because he had shot a rubber band at the picture of naked baby angels hung up in their classroom. He had hit one right on its plump little bottom. Marcia almost giggled now, remembering.

"Rembrandt. The greatest portraitist of all time. Look at this woman. Thick neck. Bulbous nose. Wrinkled jowls. Sunken eyes. Is she ugly?"

Marcia studied the picture. She had never really looked at a famous portrait before. "No."

"Why not? This isn't some twenty-year-old babe in a bikini that Rembrandt painted."

"She's—well, you can tell that she's a nice person."

" 'Nice'?" Mr. Morrison twisted his lip in disdain at the word. Ms. Singpurwalla didn't let them use "nice" in their writing, either.

"That she has a good heart. She's kind. And she's lived a long time, and her life has been hard—like, maybe she lost a child, or her husband died . . ." Marcia thought of the sad-eyed woman at the nursing home. "And maybe she has a daughter who never comes to see her, but she loves her daughter anyway, and she, like, never gives up hoping that she *will* come to see her."

Marcia stopped. She was sounding like Lizzie!

"All that from one portrait," Mr. Morrison said. "If a hundred people looked at this portrait, they'd tell a hundred different stories. *This* is the portrait of a beautiful woman."

"How did he do it? How did Rembrandt do it?"

Mr. Morrison's laugh was bitter. "If I knew the answer to that, I probably wouldn't be teaching in a suburban middle school whose art budget has been cut for the third year in a row."

Marcia walked slowly back to her desk. Mr. Morrison was standing in the aisle, apparently still lost in his own thoughts, when Marcia said, "Can I show you something?"

"Sure."

Marcia opened her French notebook to the picture of Madame Cowper. She had almost ripped it up into tiny little pieces and thrown it away, but something had made her save it.

Mr. Morrison stifled a chuckle. "Don't tell me she saw this."

Marcia still couldn't laugh about it. She nodded mutely.

"What'd she say?"

"Something about how I draw very well, and it was an accurate picture, but it wasn't very kind."

"What do *you* think?"

"That she was right. I didn't mean for her to see it."

"All right, Miss Marcia Faitak. When we finish with still lifes, we're going to try some portraits. Your assignment is to find the ugliest person you can and show his or her inner beauty. Start looking for a model."

So Mr. Morrison was telling her, thirteen-year-old Marcia Faitak, to be another Rembrandt. Who was he kidding? But something about the assignment made her pulse quicken. She knew where she could find a model, a whole building full of models.

West Creek Manor Nursing Home.

At Marcia's next visit to the nursing home, on Wednesday, she wanted to find out whether the southern-talking man from Nashville, Tennessee, had been impressed by Mavis Getty's dark red fingernails and soft green eye shadow. But she and Lizzie were assigned to a Miss Alberta Estes.

"*Miss*," Marcia said to Lizzie as they walked down the long corridor to find the right room.

"Well, Emily Dickinson never married, either," Lizzie said, sounding a bit defensive.

"Emily who?"

"Dickinson. The poet?"

Marcia shrugged. All right, there were *two* old maids for her to feel sorry for.

She knew she would regret asking her next question,

but she couldn't stop herself. "You aren't going— Has anyone— Has anyone asked you to the eighth-grade dance?"

Lizzie blushed. Red-haired people shouldn't blush, Marcia thought crossly. Red hair *and* red skin was not a flattering combination. "Actually, two boys asked me."

Yes, Marcia regretted her question all right.

"Tom asked me first, and I'm starting to like Tom. He's on the math team, too, and he writes for the magazine, and we have a lot in common. So I told Tom I'd go with him, and then guess who asked me?"

Marcia refused to guess. She would die if it was Alex, just shrivel up inside and die.

"Ethan! Remember how I used to have that crush on him?"

Overcome with relief, Marcia managed a small smile. "Slightly."

Lizzie laughed. "Oh, I know I made it pretty obvious. I think the whole school knew. Poor Ethan! I still have about a hundred poems I wrote to him, back in sixth grade. My poetry has improved a *lot* since then, let me tell you. If the best you can do for a rhyme with 'Ethan' is 'heathen,' you should stick to free verse. Anyway, Ethan asked me to the dance. And all I could think was, if only I could see sixth-grade Lizzie again, just for ten seconds, and tell her! But of course I had to turn him down. He didn't look crushed or anything. I think he asked me for old times' sake. And because he's short, and I'm short."

Maybe two-hundred-pound Elliot Abrams would ask Marcia because he was fat and she was fat.

Marcia willed Lizzie not to do the polite thing and ask *her* now if *she* had an invitation to the dance. Lizzie was smart. Maybe, if Marcia was lucky, Lizzie would have picked up on the desperation in Marcia's voice earlier.

Lizzie hesitated, as if torn between politeness and awareness. "And you . . . ?"

"I'm forming an old maids' club," Marcia said, trying to make a joke of it. "Me, and Alberta Estes, and—who's that poet?"

"Emily Dickinson."

"Me, and Alberta, and Emily."

"Marcia Faitak, all you have to do is lift your pinkie, and every boy in our school would come crawling to your feet."

Ha! But it felt good to have Lizzie say it. Marcia lifted her pinkie high in the air and waited expectantly.

Nothing happened, except that Lizzie laughed.

Then Marcia noticed Alex and a boy named Todd approaching. Did she want to say hello to him, or would it be too painful?

"Come on, Lizzie." She and Lizzie started down the hall.

"Hey, Marcia!" Alex called after her. She let him catch up with them. "How's it going? So they put you and Lizzie together? Todd and I are supposed to be playing chess with these two guys. Do you know how many men they have in this place? Two. A thousand women, and two men. So we have to play chess with them every single time. At least they're not senile."

"Were they in the hall when we came for orientation?" Marcia asked.

"Yup. That's them. Watching every girl in sight. When Todd and I showed up on Monday, they practically keeled over with disappointment."

"There's another non-senile man," Marcia said. "He's new. From Nashville, Tennessee."

"How do you know so much?" It was flattering that he was ignoring Lizzie and Todd completely and focusing entirely on her.

She made her eyes big and wide. "I have my ways. But if you see him, tell him—well, don't tell him anything, but maybe mention the name Mavis Getty, and see what he says."

Alex grinned at her. "Check." He and Todd turned into the room of one of the chess players.

Now Marcia was the matchmaker for Sarah and Travis *and* for Mavis Getty and the man from Nashville. Who was going to play matchmaker for her?

Alberta Estes was tiny, one of the few women Marcia had ever seen who needed to *gain* weight. She looked like a bird. Her blue eyes were bright and darting, and her hands picked constantly at a balled tissue, shredding it into tiny wisps, as if she were preparing a soft lining for her nest.

Miss Estes, too, was thrilled at the idea of a makeover. "Oh, my!" she said. "I'm going to feel like one of those Hollywood movie stars. Do you girls know that I've never worn makeup in my life? Not even one speck of lipstick?"

"Why not?" Marcia asked, rummaging in her bag for the shade she already knew she wanted: First Kiss Pink.

"My mother died when I was four years old, and I was raised by my father and my three older brothers, on our farm on the Plains."

Lizzie was busy scribbling in her notebook.

"They didn't know anything more about girls than the man in the moon. I never had a pretty dress until the war came, and I earned the money for it myself, working in a munitions plant outside Denver. But I was too old by then to have the knack for dolling myself up. I've always worn my hair in this same bun. And I've never known how to put any of that stuff on my face."

"Today is the day, then!" Marcia said. "Is it okay if I take down the bun?"

Miss Estes's hands flew to her hair, and her eyes darted fearfully toward the mirror across from her bed. Then: "Why not?" she said.

"Tell us more about the farm," Lizzie prompted. "Where did you go to school?"

"A one-room schoolhouse, two miles down the road. I

walked there and back by myself, when I was six years old. My brothers were over at the regional high school. So I walked by myself, a little bit of a thing in a feed-sack dress."

Marcia began combing out Miss Estes's hair. It was long and white and incredibly soft, like spun silk the color of moonlight. Marcia could tell that if it weren't so long, it would have some natural curl to it. But she didn't know how to cut hair, and she knew without asking that Miss Estes wouldn't want it cut.

Miss Estes talked on, telling Lizzie about the hard work on the farm—the endless battle against dust and dirt and grinding poverty. The only time in her life that she had ever escaped from the farm was during the three wartime years that she worked in the factory.

"Oh, the fun we had!"

But after the war she had gone back home to keep house for her father and her remaining brother. One brother had married; the other had been killed on D-day, during World War II.

"Why didn't you ever marry?" Marcia asked, even though it was Lizzie's job to do the interview.

"Who would have taken care of Pa and Bill?"

"They could have taken care of themselves!" Marcia answered indignantly. Miss Estes just smiled.

She looked so pretty when Marcia was finished—her eyes accented by blue eye shadow, her lips pink, her hair falling past her shoulders like a bridal veil. Too pretty to be the model for Marcia's "ugly but beautiful" portrait. Maybe Alberta Estes deserved the man from Nashville? But Mrs. Getty had spoken for him first.

Lizzie was thanking Miss Estes and putting her notebook away.

"Were you—were you happy?" Marcia suddenly blurted out.

"Oh, yes," Alberta Estes said. "I've had a wonderful life. And this has been a wonderful day."

nine

Next Monday's lady was as opposite from Alberta Estes as two ninety-year-old ladies in a nursing home could be. Mrs. Agnes Applebaum looked up with a scowl when Lizzie and Marcia presented themselves at the door of her room.

"Who in blazes are you?" she barked at them.

"I'm Marcia Faitak, and she's Lizzie Archer," Marcia told her. She didn't need her tote of Jay-Dub samples this time. There was nothing that would improve Agnes Applebaum's appearance more than a simple smile.

"We're here to visit you," Lizzie explained timidly.

Mrs. Applebaum's scowl deepened. "Why? Out of the goodness of your little hearts? Wait. I know. It's for a Girl Scout badge. Don't they have some badge for visiting the elderly? Or—you're not from a church, are you? Handing out Bibles to help us get ready to meet our Maker? When I meet mine, I have a thing or two to tell Him that isn't in any Bible."

"We're from West Creek Middle School," Marcia said. Somehow she knew that wouldn't appease Agnes Applebaum.

"Why aren't you home doing your schoolwork? I know, this *is* your schoolwork. And they wonder why kids today can't read or write or do a simple sum. Because they're off bothering people in nursing homes who are waiting to die in peace."

"Maybe we should come back another time?" Lizzie offered.

Agnes Applebaum laughed. To Marcia's surprise, the laugh didn't sound altogether hostile. "When? Do you think I'm like this only on Mondays? That on Tuesdays I'm a lovable old grannie with a twinkle in her eye?"

Marcia decided to try a more direct approach. "Do you want us to go?"

Mrs. Applebaum considered the question. Then she gave an exaggerated sigh. "If this is your schoolwork, you might as well do it. If you don't, it'll be something else they can blame me for. And they'll send in some social worker from the county to find out why I'm not more 'cooperative.' No, come on in. Make yourselves at home. Both of you."

Marcia and Lizzie entered the room and perched themselves on the edge of Mrs. Applebaum's bed. She'd probably yell at them for it, but there wasn't any other place to sit.

"All right, what can I do for you? Don't tell me. You"—she pointed at Lizzie—"you're here to record all my *fascinating* stories in your notebook and then send them off to the West Creek Historical Society to preserve for posterity. You're going to ask me if I peed in a privy and made my clothes out of burlap feed sacks. And *you*"—she pointed at Marcia—"you're going to smear some crud on my wrinkled old face and tell me how bee-you-ti-ful I look, not a *day* over eighty-five. Am I right?"

Marcia looked at Lizzie. Lizzie's freckles stood out vividly against her pale skin. Suddenly Marcia felt angry. It might not be any fun to be Agnes Applebaum, but it wasn't all that much fun to spend time with her, either.

"Come on, Lizzie, let's go," she said.

"Girls!" Mrs. Applebaum's voice was booming, commanding. "I already told you that I want you to stay."

She certainly had a funny way of showing it. And what if Marcia and Lizzie didn't want to stay? "Then why are you making fun of us?" Marcia asked, still too angry to be polite.

"Marcia," Lizzie cautioned.

"Do you think we *want* to be doing this? And for your information, after my makeovers, every single person looked a thousand times better. And the stories they told Lizzie *were* extremely interesting, and not one of them was about a privy."

Agnes Applebaum laughed again. She was less grim-looking when she laughed. "Girls, I apologize. Ever since I broke my hip for the *second* time last summer and had to come here, I've been somewhat—what's the word? Not *cranky*, but . . . Oh, cranky's probably close enough."

"Would you rather we didn't do the interview? And

the makeover?" Lizzie asked. "We could talk about other things."

"The weather!" Mrs. Applebaum sounded even crankier than before. "Let's talk about the weather! Fascinating subject! The people here never tire of it. Would you say this summer was hotter or cooler than the summer of thirty-three?"

"Hotter," Marcia said. Two could play at Mrs. Applebaum's game.

"But you two were in the pool all summer, I suppose."

"No," Marcia told her. "I wasn't in the pool because my ankle was in a cast." Mrs. Applebaum wasn't the only one in the world with a broken bone.

"How did you break your ankle?" Mrs. Applebaum asked.

"In seventh grade we have to go to outdoor ed. You know, you go away for a few days with your whole class and stay in a smelly cabin and go on these horrible hikes in the pouring rain? Well, maybe you don't know, but that's what they made us do. And this boy, Alex? He pretended to be a rattlesnake. He had brought this real snake rattle with him. And Lizzie and I heard it and started running down the trail—wouldn't you run if you heard a snake rattle right where you were sitting?—and I tripped on a stupid rock, and fell, and that's how I broke my ankle."

"Tell me more about this boy, Alex."

"He's just a boy." Marcia felt herself flushing.

"Just a boy who pretends to be a rattlesnake."

"It wasn't like he had to pretend all that hard," Marcia said.

"She likes him," Mrs. Applebaum said to Lizzie. "And he likes her. But the course of true love isn't running smoothly. Am I right?"

Lizzie had the good sense not to say anything. Marcia wasn't about to say anything, either.

"Let me give you some advice."

Marcia waited, curious as to what Mrs. Applebaum would say. Maybe she *would* have some good advice to offer. Whatever else she was, she wasn't dumb.

"Snakes are for the most part shy and timid creatures. That is the point of the rattle, after all, to scare you away. They want to scare you, because they're scared of *you*. Tell me, you, the meek and mild one, is he scared of her?"

Lizzie looked imploringly at Marcia, but Marcia didn't help her out.

"No," Lizzie finally said. "I don't think so."

"Think again," said Agnes Applebaum.

Was Alex scared of her? What was there to be scared about? Marcia took a walk the next day, by herself, over toward Alex's house. She wasn't walking *to* his house, she told herself, just in its general direction. She took her sketch pad with her, in case she saw some terrific-looking autumn tree. "See?" she could say to Alex, "I wasn't thinking about you, I was thinking about art."

If only the leaves on Marcia's stupid tree would turn color, fall off, and be ready for raking! Then Alex would come over to rake them, and remember toilet-papering the tree, and fall in love with her all over again. Unless he had never liked her at all and had T.P.ed her tree only to impress his friends. But why T.P. *her* tree? Did boys T.P. trees of girls they were afraid of?

Halfway to Alex's house, Marcia saw the perfect tree for sketching. Unlike Marcia's tree, this one was almost completely bare, its gaunt branches reaching toward the sky like stiff, arthritic fingers. One scarlet leaf—just one—clung to the topmost branch, impossibly bright against the blue Colorado sky. "I am not dead yet," the leaf was saying.

Marcia sat down on a curb and began drawing.

Five minutes later, Alex Ryan sat down next to her.

Marcia's breath quickened, but she didn't stop drawing, or acknowledge his presence in any way. Finally she colored the one flaming leaf. *Look at me, notice me, ask me to the dance,* the leaf was saying now.

"You *are* good," Alex said as she began putting her scattered colored pencils back into the box.

Marcia tried to think of something flirtatious to say in return, but instead she said, "Thanks." Maybe Alex was frightened by flirtation? But he had never seemed frightened of it before.

"Are you surviving Morrison?" Alex asked.

"Yeah. At first it was—it was like he hated everything

I did. Everything we all did. But especially me. But now I think he just expects a lot. Which is sort of good, I guess. I mean, I'm getting better. A lot better. I never used to be able to draw like this."

"What about Williams? Every time I see you and Lizzie at the nursing home, you're in with some old lady, yakking away like you've known each other forever."

Marcia hadn't realized that Alex had been watching her at the nursing home, noticing her interactions with the residents there. The thought was sweet and unsettling.

"It's not as bad as I thought it would be. The old people Lizzie and I have talked to have been pretty nice." She remembered in the nick of time that boys like to talk about themselves. And she had to make sure to work in some remark about her broken ankle and call Alex a big brute or a hairy beast again. "What about *you*? Do you mind playing chess with them?"

Alex thought for a moment before he replied. "Not really. It's not like it's the worst thing in my life, or anything. Oh, I met the third non-senile guy, the southern dude. He's definitely on the ball. He even beat me a couple of times, and I'm good."

"Who taught you to play?" Marcia hoped it was a safe question, though maybe it would be safer to talk about running or football or some manly sport. Not many hairy beasts played chess.

"My dad."

Marcia had seen Alex's dad. He was a tall, handsome,

broad-shouldered, clean-cut man who looked a lot like Alex.

"You look a lot like him," Marcia said tentatively.

"I do?" Alex sounded less than thrilled by the comparison.

"I mean, you're both tall, and you have broad shoulders, and look like you're good in sports." Marcia opened her eyes extra wide, with the same yearning look she had wasted the other day on Travis Edwards.

"I'm okay at sports, I guess," Alex muttered.

"I used to be better at sports, before I broke my ankle," Marcia said. She held her foot out in front of him, hoping that it looked delicate and dainty. Her shoe was a tiny size five. If only she had worn her thin silver ankle bracelet.

Alex looked away. Maybe the thin silver ankle bracelet wouldn't have made any difference, anyway.

There was an awkward moment of silence, then Alex jumped to his feet. "See you around," he said.

A sudden cold gust of wind made Marcia shiver. She looked back at the tree she had sketched. The wind had snatched the last bright leaf from its clutching branch. The leaf was gone.

Marcia still hadn't started drawing any of the people at the nursing home. *Find the ugliest person you can and paint his or her inner beauty.* The problem was that once you got to know them, none of the people at West Creek Manor looked ugly. The sad-eyed lady looked sad, Mavis Getty was fat, with clown hair, Alberta Estes was a plain old maid, Agnes Applebaum had a half century of frown lines, but none of them was *ugly*, really. Marcia decided to try drawing all of them.

Next, she and Lizzie were assigned to visit the sad-eyed lady, Mrs. Mabel Thompson.

"I don't think I can do this," Lizzie whispered to Marcia. "*Tape*-record her while she tells us how her son was killed in Vietnam and she still misses him every day?"

"I know," Marcia said. "It's like, she needs a whole life makeover."

They had almost reached Mrs. Thompson's door. "But everyone is here because they have nobody," Marcia realized. "It isn't like anybody here has a terrific life. Let's just go in there like we did for everybody else."

Mrs. Thompson was sitting in a chair, a real chair, not a wheelchair, waiting for them.

"Hi, Mrs. Thompson!" Marcia said with forced cheerfulness. "We told you we'd come back to see you, and here we are!"

Mrs. Thompson looked confused. "You told me? You'd come back to see me?" It was obvious that she didn't remember the previous visit at all.

Marcia let it go. "I'm Marcia Faitak, from West Creek Middle School."

"I'm Lizzie Archer," Lizzie managed to say.

"We're here to interview you for a school project," Marcia went on, "and . . ." She didn't think she could go through with the makeover this time. "And I'd like to draw a picture of you, if you don't mind."

"Draw a picture? Of me?" Mrs. Thompson still sounded confused. But then she seemed to understand. "Of course, if you want to." She pointed to the wall of photographs. "I have some pictures I'd like to show you, too."

Uh-oh.

"This is my son, Robbie," Mrs. Thompson said. "Here he is as a baby. He was killed in Vietnam. October eighteenth, nineteen sixty-seven. That was the day he died."

Marcia was afraid Lizzie would start to cry, but Lizzie actually recovered first.

"What was he like as a little boy?" Lizzie asked. "Is it all right if I tape-record this?"

Mrs. Thompson nodded.

"Did he do anything funny? Or naughty? In the picture he looks as if he might have been mischievous."

Mrs. Thompson settled back into her chair. She wasn't smiling exactly, but something in her face relaxed. "I'll say he was mischievous. One Christmas, he must have been four years old, he found all the presents I had wrapped and hidden from him, in that tiny bit of an apartment we had over on Fourth Street, and the next thing I knew, he had opened them all. A week before Christmas! We didn't have a single present left to give him on Christmas Day."

Marcia was sketching as quickly as she could, her fingers flying over the page with her pencil.

"What did you do?" Lizzie asked.

"What *could* I do? I took my last dollar and went to the dime store and bought a pack of crayons, a coloring book, a couple of those tiny toy cars, and a stick of candy or two, and that was what Santa brought him on Christmas morning. And he was as pleased with that cheap stuff as he had been with the fire engine and the Tinkertoy kit. Friendly fire was what killed him, in Vietnam. He was killed by mistake by his own side."

Lizzie shot an anguished glance at Marcia. "What was he like at school?" She choked out the question.

"Oh, I pitied the poor woman who was Robbie's kindergarten teacher," Mrs. Thompson said. "The very first day—the very first day—he ran away at recess, following an ice cream truck he heard going by . . ."

With Lizzie's gentle prompting, Mrs. Thompson told them story after story as Marcia worked on her picture: of a pretty old lady with a pale smile hovering about her lips, and sad, sad eyes.

ten

The dance was exactly two weeks away. Sarah had stopped asking Marcia whether she should wear her new glitter eye shadow to it. In fact, she had stopped mentioning the dance to Marcia altogether, which was partly a relief and partly a source of further irritation. Did Sarah really think Marcia was so sensitive that she couldn't bear to hear the word *dance* spoken in her presence?

Sarah was over at Marcia's house Friday after school, lying on Marcia's bed, going through the latest shipment of Jay-Dub samples. Marcia and Gwennie were helping at another Jay-Dub party the next day. Marcia didn't know where. Probably the house of another rich lady with a strange name who would talk the whole time about plastic surgery.

"Marcia," Sarah finally said, in her most timid voice.

Marcia stiffened. She knew Sarah was working up her nerve to utter the awful word.

"About the . . ."

"Dance," Marcia finished for her.

Sarah brightened, as if grateful that Marcia had been

the one to say it. "Do you want me to try to do something?"

"Like what? Do you have a magic wand I don't know about?"

"I could drop a hint to Travis, and then maybe he could drop a hint to Alex, and—"

"No!" Marcia shrieked. "Sarah, don't you *dare*! Boys don't *get* hints, boys can't *drop* hints. The gene for hinting is completely missing from their DNA. Sarah, promise me you won't. Promise. Promise me now."

Sarah's face bore the unmistakable stamp of guilt.

"You didn't. Oh, Sarah. What did you say to him? You have to tell me."

"*He* said, did I want to go with you and Alex, and, well, what *could* I say? So I said—" Sarah broke off.

"You said *what*?"

"That Alex hadn't exactly asked you yet."

"Great. What did Travis say then?"

"Nothing really. Just . . ."

"Just *what*?"

"Just 'I thought he liked her.' "

It was too much for Marcia. Unable to hold on to the cold comfort of pride any longer, she felt the tears rising up. "I thought he liked me, too," she whispered.

"Marcia," Sarah said solemnly, "I have an idea."

Marcia wasn't the type to let herself cry. She gave her nose one long hard blow. "If it's as good as the hinting idea, I'm not sure I want to hear it."

"It's a *great* idea. Listen. Did the grapefruit help?"

"The *grapefruit*? What does grapefruit have to do with anything? I guess it helped." Actually, Marcia hadn't thought about her weight for a while. "I've lost four pounds now. But I did a lot of walking, too, so I don't know that it was entirely from eating the grapefruit."

"Certain foods work in the human body in mysterious ways. Like, grapefruit burns up fat. Am I correct?"

"And your point is?"

"*Other* foods can work in the body in *other* mysterious ways. Can work in *other* people's bodies in mysterious ways."

"Such as?"

"Pine nuts." Sarah beamed.

"Pine nuts?"

"Pine nuts," Sarah explained, "are an aphrodisiac. You know, they make people fall in love. I read a whole article about them in one of my mother's magazines."

"What are pine nuts? Are they like pinecones?"

"No, they're . . . Well, I don't know that they're nuts, exactly, but they're sort of like nuts. You can buy them at King Soopers. Did you ever have pasta with pesto sauce? Pesto is made with pine nuts and basil. Basil is an aphrodisiac, too."

"I still don't get it," Marcia said. "I'm supposed to eat pesto, and then Alex will fall in love with me?"

"No. *Alex* has to eat it. Not pesto, necessarily. But pine nuts. *Alex* eats the pine nuts, and then he falls in love."

"With me?"

"I'm not quite sure how it works. I think he falls in love with whoever's around when he eats them."

"How many does he have to eat?"

"I don't think there's any set amount. The more the better?"

Marcia burst out laughing. "Sarah, you're crazy!"

Sarah laughed, too. "I'm not saying it's guaranteed. But it's worth a try. It's like, what have we got to lose?"

Marcia knew the sad, true answer to that one. Nothing.

Sarah's father drove the girls to the high school football game that night. It was the second home game of the season. Marcia had missed the first one because at the last moment she had seen a pimple coming on her chin and decided that, anyway, she was too fat to go.

Now it felt wonderful to be climbing to the top of the bleachers on a clear, cold night, carrying a heavy blue blanket that exactly matched the color of her eyes, her West Creek High red-and-gold pompons, and a small plastic bag full of pine nuts. Sarah had found them in her kitchen at home; her dad was a gourmet cook with lots of exotic ingredients on hand.

"Did he ask you what you wanted them for?" Marcia asked Sarah as they settled themselves on the highest bleacher to wait for the other eighth graders, including, Marcia hoped, Alex.

"No, I didn't tell him I was taking them. It would have been, you know, sort of hard to explain? We can buy him a new bag if we use these all up."

"Sarah?"

"Uh-huh?"

"How exactly are we going to get Alex to eat them?"

"That's your part," Sarah said. "My part was getting them to you; your part is getting them to Alex."

"Getting them *into* Alex."

Sarah giggled, but Marcia could tell that Sarah's attention was elsewhere. She was obviously scanning the crowd of kids trickling into the stadium for any sign of Travis.

Jasmine, Keeley, and Brittany joined them. Not Lizzie. Lizzie had gone to a couple of the games back in seventh grade, but she never went anymore.

"I see him!" Sarah squealed. She waved frantically until Travis noticed her and gave her a huge, happy grin as he headed up the bleachers toward where they were sitting.

Marcia's heart clenched with jealousy. If only Alex would grin that way at her. *And* come sit beside her with his arm draped casually, protectively, around her shoulders, as Travis was now doing to Sarah. Marcia fingered the bag of pine nuts in her pocket. It was going to be a long, cold, lonely night if Alex didn't show.

Then she saw him. Alex, Dave, Ethan, and Julius had arrived together. Marcia wasn't about to wave, but she didn't need to. The boys started climbing up toward them,

Alex mock-wrestling with Dave so that he sent him sprawling onto some old lady's bony lap.

"Sorry, ma'am," she heard Alex say politely. "My friend here has a rare illness that makes him trip and fall onto strangers."

The old lady glared at both boys.

Marcia thought quickly. She had to arrange things so that she was seated next to Alex. She couldn't be feeding him pine nuts from three rows away. And she definitely didn't want to be feeding him pine nuts only to have him fall in love with somebody else who by an accident of fate happened to be sitting closer to him.

Right now Marcia was wedged between Jasmine, Keeley, and Brittany, on one side, and Sarah and Travis, on the other, the worst possible place to be. Without offering any explanation, she got up and moved to the other side of Travis, knowing that Sarah, at least, would understand. Now she had to hope she would get Alex next to her instead of one of the other boys.

Dave was ahead of Alex, coming up the aisle, so that meant he'd be the one to sit closest to Marcia. Well, maybe she'd feed pine nuts to both boys and see who fell in love with her first. Sure enough, Dave plopped himself down next to Marcia, with Alex next to Dave, and Ethan and Julius next to Alex. Maybe Marcia would go ahead and feed pine nuts to everybody.

"Hey," Dave said to Marcia.

"Hey," Marcia said back.

Alex turned toward her. "Been drawing any more trees lately?"

Marcia took a chance. "Speaking of trees, the one at my house is going to be losing its leaves pretty soon."

Alex looked puzzled at the remark, as if he had forgotten all about Marcia's tree: the toilet paper, the broken branch, the promise to rake, everything. How could something that had meant so much to her mean so little to him?

She wished she had never made the remark now, but she'd sound like a lunatic if she didn't explain. Before she could say anything more, Alex apparently made the connection himself. "Whoopee," he said glumly. "Thanks for reminding me."

"But it's my leaves you'll be raking," Marcia wanted to say, "and I'll be right there beside you, helping." Stung by his response, she looked away, only to see Travis running his fingers through Sarah's short blond hair.

It was pine nuts or nothing now.

Dave gave her the perfect opportunity. "I'm starving," he complained. "Do we have time to head down to the snack bar before the kickoff?"

Marcia pulled out her plastic bag. "I have some pine nuts. Anybody want some? Dave? *Alex?*"

Dave squinted down at the bag suspiciously. "What do they taste like?"

"They're good," Marcia said. She should have tried one herself, earlier, but she hadn't wanted to fall in love with the wrong person by mistake. In *A Midsummer Night's Dream*, Titania the Fairy Queen fell in love by mistake with this guy named Bottom—that was really his name—who had a pair of donkey's ears growing out of his head. What if Marcia had started munching away on pine nuts and then fallen in love by mistake with Elliot Abrams?

"They're nutty," Marcia went on, "and piney. Try one."

Dave held out his hand. To her relief, Alex held out his hand, too, and so did Ethan and Julius. It was funny to see them sitting there, all in a row, with their hands outstretched.

Marcia poured a small pile of pine nuts into Dave's hand, and then a huge overflowing heap into Alex's hand. "Oops," she said lightly. Then she poured a few each for Ethan and Julius. She waited while each boy chewed and swallowed his allotment. Alex swallowed all of his!

"What do you think?" Marcia asked.

"They're okay," Dave said. "Sort of greasy, maybe." He held out his hand for more.

"Alex?"

He shook his head. "I'm fine."

Marcia carefully doled out two more pine nuts to Dave. He stared down at his hand, seemingly surprised that his second helping was so stingy. Then Marcia put the bag back into her pocket. So far, so good. But now she had to make sure that Alex's attention was on her, and not on the cheerleaders down on the field. Luckily, Dave, still hungry after his pine nut snack, wandered off in search of other refreshments.

"Alex?"

He turned his head. "Yeah?"

"Did you hear what Ms. Williams said about Oktoberfest?"

"It's something at the nursing home, right?"

"She said it's a big thing down there—all the residents go. She wants the West Creek kids to think of something special to do for it. It's next Saturday, a week from tomorrow."

And the dance is two weeks from tonight.

Alex grinned. "I guess I could yodel and wear lederhosen."

Marcia laughed. It was the friendliest thing he had said so far that evening. Were the pine nuts starting to work already?

"Maybe we could—I don't know—get together some time and plan something out?"

As soon as she said it, she hated herself. Talk about a flimsy pretext for spending time with a boy! She had always scorned girls who stooped so low as to call a boy, pretending that they needed a homework assignment. But then again, desperate times called for desperate measures.

Alex hesitated. "Maybe sometime. Not tomorrow." He gave an exaggerated groan.

The hesitation was worrisome, but the groan was somehow encouraging. "What's happening tomorrow?"

"My mom is having a party."

"That doesn't sound so bad."

"It's not just any old party. This one's for ladies to come over and try on makeup, and perfume, and stuff like that."

It couldn't be. But it had to be. Was the Jay-Dub party Marcia and Gwennie were helping with tomorrow at *Alex's* house? Was this the worst possible thing that could happen, or the best?

"And my mom wants me to be the *butler*. To answer the door, wearing a *tie*, and take everybody's coats." Alex groaned again.

"I'm going to be there, too," Marcia confessed. "My mom's the one who's running the party, and I always help her with them."

Something flickered in Alex's eyes. Horror? Or amusement? "The butler and the butlerette," he said.

"Shut up, you two. It's the kickoff." Dave, back from his expedition to the snack bar, whacked Alex goodnaturedly on the shoulder.

Marcia sat back to watch the first half. She had done what she could. She'd offer Alex more pine nuts at halftime and hope for the best. *The butler and the butlerette.* It had possibilities.

eleven

Marcia slept till nine on Saturday. Then she confronted her mother in the kitchen.

"The Jay-Dub party today—whose house is it at?"

Her mother looked surprised that Marcia wanted to know. "Elaine Ryan's, right here in West Creek. Doesn't she have a son who goes to school with you?"

"*Alex* Ryan," Marcia snapped.

"Oh, the boy who damaged the tree. The boy with the snake rattle." For an instant her mother looked worried, then her forehead magically uncreased again. "Well, his mother seems perfectly lovely. It goes to show that even the most caring parents . . ."

Her mother was missing the point altogether. First of all, Alex wasn't some kind of juvenile delinquent, whose parents had suffered terrible disappointment in him. Second, it should have occurred to her mother that Marcia might be embarrassed to be helping at a Jay-Dub party at the house of a boy she liked.

"Don't you think you should have asked me first?"

"Asked you what?"

"If you can do a party at the house of one of my friends?"

"Oh, honey, *his* mother approached *me* about doing the party. I'm sure Alex couldn't care less about something like this. You know how boys are, utterly oblivious to anything that doesn't concern them."

"It does concern him. He's going to be helping today, too."

"All the better," her mother said encouragingly. "Maybe he's turning himself around." Suddenly Marcia's mother looked at Marcia, really looked at her. "Are you saying that this boy is someone special?"

It was probably Marcia's own fault that her mother didn't know about Alex. Marcia was always telling everything to Gwennie and Sarah and her other friends; she hardly ever talked to her own mother anymore. What if she said now, "Yes, he's someone special, and the dance is less than two weeks away, and he still hasn't asked me yet?"

"Sort of," Marcia said.

"Well, wear your new blue sweater. Blue is definitely your color. Have you lost weight? Your figure is looking very nice again. That little tummy bulge is almost completely gone now."

Marcia had been about to make herself a piece of cinnamon toast, dripping with melted butter and heaping spoonfuls of cinnamon sugar. Instead she rummaged in the crisper for the last grapefruit.

"Thanks," she said.

• • •

Marcia called Gwennie right after breakfast to tell her. At first there was a long pause as Gwennie digested the news.

"He's probably more embarrassed than you are," Gwennie said. "And sometimes you feel closer to someone after you've been through something like this together. The two of you can start a support group for survivors of Jay-Dub parties."

Gwennie's laugh made Marcia laugh, too. She told Gwennie Alex's "butler and butlerette" remark.

"Perfect! It sounds like he has the right attitude here. And now I'll get to meet him, too. We'll both be able to observe him in his natural habitat."

"Gwennie?"

"What?"

"What if he never asks me to the dance?"

There was another long pause. "We'll know more after today. And if he doesn't ask you, we'll start working on Plan B."

"The plan where I sit at home all by myself in my ratty old bathrobe and do my nails?"

"The plan where you have a terrific evening, dance or no dance, and wonder why you ever bothered liking a boy who didn't have the good sense to like you back. *If* he doesn't like you back. Which we don't know yet."

"Gwennie?"

"What?"

"Have you ever heard that feeding a boy pine nuts will make him fall in love with you?"

Gwennie laughed again. "No. Where did you hear that?"

"Sarah."

"Well, I guess feeding a boy anything makes him like you at least a little bit. But I wouldn't put too much faith in Sarah's pine nut theory. Why? Are you planning to feed him pine nuts at the party today?"

"I fed them to him at the football game last night."

"And? Did it work?"

"Not that I could tell. He acted about the same as always. Do you think maybe there's a delayed effect? Like, if he ate them yesterday, he'll fall in love with me today?"

"I think you're crazy, and Sarah's even crazier. And if Alex doesn't ask you to this dance, then he's the craziest of all."

At his house, Alex answered the doorbell, wearing his jacket and tie, looking extremely handsome. Marcia was glad she had worn her blue sweater.

"Come in," he said politely. "Can I help you carry anything?"

"Yes, dear, thank you," Marcia's mother said. "There are seven more cartons in the back of the van, plus two folding card tables." She shot Marcia a glance of approval. It was plain that she realized now that you shouldn't judge a boy entirely on the basis of one toilet-papered tree and one snake impersonation.

"He is *cute*," Gwennie whispered.

Alex looked even cuter than usual as he started carrying in the cartons, two at a time. When he stacked a second heavy carton on top of the first one, he grinned at Marcia, as if to make sure she was impressed with him. She was.

"Be careful, dear," Marcia's mother said. "You don't want to hurt your back."

"The Ryan family butler is very strong, ma'am," he replied.

When her mother was out of hearing, Marcia whispered to him daringly, "She should have seen what you carried down a trail once." It had been the most romantic moment of her life, when Alex and Dave had carried her back to the cabin after her accident at outdoor ed. Unfortunately, she had been in too much pain at the time to savor it to its fullest. Did Alex also remember the romance of it?

He didn't reply. You'd think at least he'd make some crack about how heavy a load she had been. Marcia didn't particularly want to hear any well-worded jokes about her weight, but it was almost worse to have Alex say nothing.

Back inside, Alex's mother came bustling over to greet them. She was very pretty—slim and young-looking, with the merest hint of makeup on her eyelids.

"Kathy!" She gave Marcia's mother a welcoming hug. "And your two gorgeous girls. The three of you look like sisters."

Marcia's mother looked pleased at that remark.

To Marcia, Mrs. Ryan added, "I can see why my son is so smitten."

Is he? Then why isn't he asking me to the dance? Did Alex's mother mean her comment to be taken seriously? Or was she just trying to give everyone some kind of friendly compliment? Marcia didn't think she and Gwennie and her mother looked like sisters.

Alex's father walked into the living room. He and Alex definitely did look alike, however much Alex had bristled at Marcia's comment about their resemblance: same broad-shouldered build, same closely cropped light brown hair.

As Alex carried in the second card table, Mr. Ryan called out, "Easy there! Watch the paint on the doorways!"

Alex's pleasant, obliging butler's grin disappeared. And, sure enough, although he had carried in everything else without any problem whatsoever, one edge of the card table did bump into the wall by the front entryway, and yes, it left a noticeable chip in the paint.

"Teenagers," his father said, to no one in particular. "The more you talk, the less they listen. It must be great to be thirteen and know absolutely everything."

Alex's mother turned to Alex's father. "I think we have everything under control here." She spoke pleasantly, but it was clear to Marcia that she was trying to get Mr. Ryan to leave.

Mr. Ryan turned to the assembled ladies to make a speech before departing. "I don't see how any of you could possibly be made lovelier than you already are," he said, with an apparent attempt at gallantry. "My son and I are both already blinded by the beauty bursting upon us. I should say, my son is *especially* blinded, right, Alex?"

He winked at Marcia. And then he was gone. Marcia shot a quick glance at Alex, but he was staring down at his feet.

"Let's check on the snacks," Gwennie announced brightly.

Marcia and Gwennie headed to the kitchen, followed by Marcia's mother, who immediately began gushing over the gorgeous trays of refreshments that Alex's mother had prepared. "Gwennie, Marcia, come look!" She popped one small shrimp into her mouth. "What was this marinated in?"

Alex's mother brightened at the question. "Some olive oil, and a hint of red wine vinegar, and some pine nuts."

Marcia and Gwennie exploded into giggles. The two mothers looked puzzled, which made the girls laugh even harder.

"Girls," Marcia's mother said again, more sternly this time. "The guests will be here in ten minutes, and we still have a lot to do."

Marcia and Gwennie started the familiar routine of setting up the makeup mirrors and arranging the display tables. When the doorbell rang for the first guests, Alex reappeared and opened the door for them. Marcia noticed, to her amusement, that he had swiped a pair of false eyelashes from one of the display tables and stuck them on his own large brown eyes.

She made herself approach him in between rings of the doorbell. "Hi, butler," she said softly. "I like your eyelashes."

He smiled. "Hi, butlerette. I like yours, too."

The wonders of Jay-Dub mascara, lavishly applied.

"Great game last night," Marcia said, to say something. West Creek High had won, 24 to 14.

"Yeah," Alex agreed. Then he hesitated. "Those snacks you were handing out? Those greasy nut things?"

Marcia swallowed. "The pine nuts?"

"Did your stomach feel all right last night? I felt kind of nauseous."

So not only had the pine nuts not made Alex fall in love, they had made him feel like throwing up. Marcia would have to give them the prize for "Sarah's worst idea ever."

"Me too," Marcia said awkwardly. Maybe he could take it as another basis for a bond between them: the butler and the butlerette, both with long eyelashes and stomach trouble from eating pine nuts. Or maybe not.

The doorbell rang again. Alex sprang into action. Marcia retreated to the display table where Gwennie was explaining to one lady the miraculous effect of "Baby Skin" wrinkle cream.

The lady studied the label. "I know I'm postponing the inevitable. I'm long overdue to have my eyes done."

Marcia thought about Alberta Estes, and Mavis Getty, and Agnes Applebaum, and Mabel Thompson. They were long overdue to get their eyes done, too. But they were beautiful, anyway.

"Your eyes look fine!" Marcia blurted out. Gwennie shot her a warning look. Marcia remembered that the whole point of a Jay-Dub party was to make people think that however fine they looked already, they could look still better with the help of some discounted-just-for-this-party, top-of-the-line, all-natural beauty products. "That cream works great," Marcia added lamely. "My mother uses it all the time."

"I guess if it buys me another year or two . . . You lucky girls, still decades away from your first face-lift. Let me tell you, getting old is the pits."

Marcia forced a sympathetic smile. Getting old was awful for Agnes Applebaum, but it wasn't awful for Alberta Estes. And whether or not it was awful had almost nothing to do with what you looked like outside and everything to do with what kind of person you were inside.

twelve

On the day of the Oktoberfest at West Creek Manor, Marcia went over to the nursing home an hour early so she could get "her" people ready for the big event; Lizzie was going to meet them all at the party. As none of the West Creek kids could think of anything better, they had decided, in an after-school meeting the previous week, that the Oktoberfest was going to be a dance, with music provided by the West Creek Middle School jazz band. Other kids were there early to move the tables out of the dining room and decorate it with a harvest theme: corn shocks, hay bales, and pumpkins.

Marcia had plotted out her route from room to room. She visited Mavis Getty first, because her appearance mattered the most. This time Mrs. Getty was waiting for her. "Yoo-hoo! Diana!" she shouted as soon as she saw Marcia coming down the hall. Marcia could see that she had put on the Autumn Flame lipstick again, but she needed another manicure.

"Why are you late?" Mrs. Getty demanded. "They told me you'd be here right at one o'clock."

"It *is* one o'clock." Marcia checked her watch. "It's one-oh-two."

"Oh-*two*," Mrs. Getty said. "At least you're here now. Come on in and shut the door. I have *so* much to tell you."

"Can I do your makeup while we talk?" Marcia asked. "And your nails? You *do* want me to do your nails, don't you?"

"*Yes*, I want you to do my nails, this is all *about* my nails. You'll never guess what happened."

"The man from Nashville!"

"Melvin. Don't you just love that name? *Mel*-vin. Well, it turns out that Melvin is quite the chess player. He's been playing up a storm with some boys, maybe you know them, nice boys, he says they are, clean-cut, real polite. So the Manor is sending him to—get this—the Creek County Seniors Chess Tournament. To represent West Creek Manor. But that's not the best part. You'll never guess the best part."

Marcia had almost finished removing the old, chipped polish. "What's the best part?"

"They told him he could bring a friend with him, a *friend*, they said."

"And he's bringing you!" Marcia crowed.

"He told them he wanted to bring 'the gal with the purty nails.' Can you believe it? Wouldn't you think the first thing a man would notice about me is my natural red hair? But no. 'The gal with the purty nails,' he said."

Shyly, from her tote bag, Marcia pulled out the portrait she had done of Mavis Getty. It had turned out surprisingly well. She had managed to capture some of the sparkle in Mrs. Getty's green eyes.

"Oh, my goodness!" Mrs. Getty said. "Is this for me? Can I put it up here on my wall?"

"If you want to."

"Of course I do! You know that other Diana, Diana number two, she told me she wishes she could put some of your pictures in that school magazine of yours."

Marcia was starting to get used to the idea, though she still hadn't dared show any of her West Creek portraits to Mr. Morrison.

"What do you think of that? Me, a pinup girl in a high school magazine! I'll have to tell Melvin." And Mrs. Getty blushed almost the same shade as her bright-red hair.

Alberta Estes looked excited about the Oktoberfest, too. She was wearing a soft blue dress that exactly matched her eyes, and she had found a plastic flower, of the same shade of blue, to tuck into her bun. Marcia decided to leave her bun alone today and concentrate on bringing out her eyes and adding some pink color to her pale lips.

Maybe the two chess players who watched all the girls would look at Alberta Estes across the room at the Oktoberfest and realize how foolish they had been to ogle girls seventy years too young for them. But Miss Estes deserved someone better.

Marcia had an inspired thought. Wasn't Mr. Adams, her math teacher, single? She was almost sure he had referred to himself once as an "old bachelor." Ancient as he was for a middle-school math teacher, he was young and dashing compared to the male West Creek Manor residents.

"When you went to the one-room school on the prairie," Marcia asked as she put the finishing touches on the eye shadow, "were you good at math?"

"Oh, yes," Alberta Estes said. "We called it arithmetic back then, and it was just simple sums, none of your fancy x's and y's. But I definitely had a head for figures. I always kept the accounts for Pa and Bill on the farm."

Marcia sighed with satisfaction. Now she needed to lure Mr. Adams out to West Creek Manor on some clever pretext. She would leave that for another day.

Mabel Thompson was sitting in her room when Marcia entered, her sad eyes looking as sad as ever.

"Are you ready for the Oktoberfest?" Marcia asked, hoping the enthusiasm she was forcing into her own voice would be contagious.

"Oktoberfest?" Mabel Thompson asked blankly.

"A big party! A dance! There's going to be live music, and everything. And I peeked at the refreshments, and they look great. Sort of German. Bratwurst—can you smell it? And squares of German chocolate cake and Black Forest cake." Four hundred calories a piece, Marcia estimated. She might have *one*, only if she absolutely couldn't resist.

"October's always been a sad month for me," Mabel said. "My son, Robbie, was killed in Vietnam in October. October eighteenth, nineteen sixty-seven. Friendly fire, they told me. Shot by mistake by his own side."

"Let me fix your hair for the party, okay?" Marcia asked. There were only so many times she could listen to the story of Mabel's son, Robbie. It would be horrible to lose a son in such a pointless, tragic way, but after hearing about it half a dozen times in the past few weeks, Marcia had to change the subject.

"Next time I come, I'm going to bring some electric curlers. Have you ever tried giving your hair more of a curl? I think it would make a big difference. Now, you sit back and relax while I see what I can do. Tell me more about Robbie. What kind of costumes did he have for Halloween?"

"He was a cowboy," Mabel said. "Every single year, he was a cowboy. I still remember the day my husband brought him home that first cowboy hat . . ."

And Mabel talked on, smiling to herself in the mirror, while Marcia gently combed her soft, wispy, white hair.

Marcia had left Agnes Applebaum until last. She greatly doubted that Mrs. Applebaum would let her "smear" any "crud" on her face or show anything but withering scorn for the Oktoberfest. But Marcia was going to try, anyway. The worst Agnes could do was bite her head off.

"Hi, Mrs. Applebaum!" Marcia greeted her. "Are you ready for the Oktoberfest?"

"No," Agnes Applebaum said. "And I suspect you knew my answer before you asked. I intend to spend the next few hours sitting peacefully in my room reading a large-print edition of one of Henry James's duller novels."

"You're not even *going* to the Oktoberfest?"

"Why on earth would I do such a thing? I can think of nothing more pathetic than watching a group of ninety-year-olds in their wheelchairs singing all the words to the 'Beer Barrel Polka.' "

"Why shouldn't they have some fun?" Marcia demanded indignantly. "Do you want everyone to be as crabby and miserable as you are?"

Agnes laughed. Marcia knew by now that feisty replies amused her. "No, but *I* plan to continue in my own crabby and miserable way, thank you. It'll be bad enough being unable to shut out the sound of the band—it's your middle-school band, correct? One shudders to think of their idea of what ninety-somethings want to hear."

Today was Marcia's day for flashes of genius. "If you come to the party, I'll introduce you to Alex, and you can see what you think of him."

Sure enough, Agnes Applebaum's eyes brightened.

"The rattlesnake boy? He still hasn't asked you to that dance of yours?"

Marcia shook her head. "I don't think he's going to."

"Have you tried whispering sweet nothings into his ear?"

"No! You're not supposed to let boys know you like them. You're supposed to tease them about things, and make them feel guilty, and call them names like 'big brute' and 'hairy beast.'"

Even as she said it, Marcia had a dawning realization. Alex didn't seem to like it when his father put him down and teased him and embarrassed him. Could he really like it all that much when Marcia did it?

"The rattlesnake strikes when he's afraid," Mrs. Applebaum reminded her. "When I was a girl—and yes, I was a girl once, a million years ago—we were told that you could catch more flies with honey than you could with vinegar. Maybe you can catch more rattlesnakes with honey, too."

Rattlesnakes, flies—what were you supposed to do with *boys*? Marcia thought now that she might have been going about things all wrong, shoving her broken ankle in Alex's face, teasing him about being a big brute and a hairy beast—though she didn't think she had ever called him "hairy beast" to his face, thank goodness. Agnes Applebaum seemed to know more about boys than the authors of all those dating-advice books put together.

"All right," Agnes said briskly, "you've intrigued me

sufficiently. I'll come to this parade of horrors, to this Ok-toberfest. Now leave me alone."

"You don't want me to fix your hair or anything, do you?"

Mrs. Applebaum shot Marcia one last baleful glance. Marcia shot her a grateful smile, and fled.

As soon as she entered the dining room, Marcia checked the room for Alex. She saw him right away, talking to Melvin-from-Nashville over by the refreshment table. Ever since the Jay-Dub party, Marcia had felt shy with Alex. It was a good thing she had made her promise to Agnes: now she had to talk to Alex, shy or not.

The West Creek Middle School jazz band was playing some really old-style tune. They sounded as good as a CD to Marcia, which proved how wrong Agnes Applebaum could be, at least about some things. Marcia still hadn't decided what she thought about Mrs. Applebaum's assessment of Alex.

Mavis Getty wheeled into the room. Marcia saw her scan the party for Melvin. Had she been that obvious when she looked for Alex? Marcia hurried over to join her.

"He's by the snack table," Marcia said by way of greeting.

Mavis laughed. "It figures. If you're looking for a man, start by finding the food."

"Aren't you hungry?" Marcia asked, smiling.

Mavis laughed again. "Now that you mention it, I am."

Alex had drifted away by the time they crossed the room. No one was dancing yet—*was* anybody going to dance? *Could* they dance, with their wheelchairs and walkers? The room was fairly crowded, though, with the residents chatting in small groups, or sitting alone listening to the music. Marcia saw Lizzie, talking with Alberta Estes and Mabel Thompson. Maybe Alberta and Mabel could become friends, the one always so cheerful and positive, the other lost in her sad memories. Alberta would be good for Mabel. Alberta Estes would be good for anyone.

At the snack table, Mavis rolled herself right up to Melvin. He was one of the few residents, male or female, who wasn't in a wheelchair. With his close-trimmed gray mustache and trim figure, he *was* a handsome man, though Marcia noticed that the two halves of his face didn't fit together perfectly. Maybe he had had a stroke, or something, on one side.

"Why, Miss Mavis, don't you look lovely," he said in a cute southern drawl.

"You're looking pretty dapper yourself, Melvin," Mavis said. "This is my friend . . ." She hesitated, plainly groping for Marcia's real name.

"Diana," Marcia said, holding out her hand.

Melvin lifted it to his lips and kissed it! Marcia managed not to giggle. No wonder he noticed ladies' fingernails!

There was an awkward silence. Marcia could tell from

Mavis's sidelong glance at the food table that she was trying to decide whether or not to eat a juicy, sizzling bratwurst in front of Melvin. It was clear she *wanted* to eat one, but not in front of her beau. Marcia remembered from *Gone With the Wind* that southern belles never ate in front of the men they were after. Most southern belles didn't weigh as much as Mrs. Getty, either.

The band started a new song, slow and romantic. Marcia took a chance. "Why don't you two dance?"

"I couldn't," Mavis breathed, gazing down at her lap. Marcia hoped that Melvin knew that meant "I'd love to."

"Miss Mavis, may I have this dance?" Melvin asked, making her a low bow.

For answer, Mavis lifted her face, radiant with happiness. Melvin took both her hands in his and gently pulled her, wheelchair and all, to the center of the dance floor. Slowly they glided in a stately circle to the music, while the other residents applauded.

Marcia scanned the dining room again, this time for Agnes Applebaum. She wasn't there, the promise-breaker!

Marcia found her back in her own room, dozing over the open book in her lap. Gently she shook her awake. "Mrs. Applebaum, it's time for the party."

Agnes glared at her. "You promised," Marcia said sternly.

"I don't recall anything about a *promise*."

"Well, you said you'd come, and it sounded like a promise to me."

"I'll come for *five* minutes."

"All right. For five minutes."

Entering the dining room, Agnes took one look at Mavis and Melvin, still dancing, and closed her eyes. "Who are those two, making a spectacle of themselves?"

"They're not making a spectacle of themselves; they're falling in love."

"It's the same thing, isn't it?"

Marcia ignored her. "Doesn't the band sound great?"

"It sounds better than I expected," Agnes admitted. "Now *you* promised something, an introduction to the rattlesnake boy. Where is he?"

"He's over there, in that group of West Creek kids."

Marcia hoped she wasn't making a terrible mistake, letting Agnes Applebaum meet Alex Ryan. How could it *not* be a terrible mistake? There was no way Agnes Applebaum wouldn't say something shocking or insulting. Even calling Alex "rattlesnake boy" would be bad enough. But it was too late now to change her mind.

When he saw her approaching, Alex left the other kids to say hello to Marcia. That was a good sign. Marcia tried to remember the rules for introducing people. Did you introduce the young person to the old person? Or the old person to the young person?

"Mrs. Applebaum, I'd like you to meet my friend Alex Ryan." Alex shook Mrs. Applebaum's hand politely. Marcia was relieved to see he was using his best butler manners. But it was Mrs. Applebaum's manners she was worried about.

"I hear you're a fine chess player," Mrs. Applebaum said.

Marcia let out her breath. She had been afraid Mrs. Applebaum was going to say, "I hear you're a fine snake rattler." Or "I hear you haven't asked this girl to your school dance."

"Thank you," Alex said.

Agnes gestured toward Mavis and Melvin. "What do you think of that, young man? Old folks out there making fools of themselves, dancing?"

Alex shot Marcia a nervous look: *What am I supposed to say now?* "Well, that's what people do at dances, isn't it?" he ventured. "Dance?"

Mrs. Applebaum pinned him with her sharp eyes. "*Is* it? Then why aren't *you* dancing?"

"I—uh—just got here."

"*They* just got here, too."

Alex looked helplessly at Marcia. Then he held out his hand.

The residents had clapped when Mavis and Melvin began dancing. When Marcia and Alex began dancing, they cheered.

"We look like idiots," Alex muttered to Marcia. It would have helped if they had known the steps to whatever dance they were supposed to be doing. Waltz? Foxtrot? Instead, they shuffled back and forth in time to the music.

Marcia didn't care. It felt so good to have Alex's right hand on the small of her back, and his left hand holding hers. "It doesn't matter how we look," she whispered back.

The silence between them felt comfortable this time. Marcia let it go on for a few moments, then she said, "Alex?"

"Uh-huh?"

"Thanks."

"For what?"

"For putting up with Agnes Applebaum. And for being so nice to Melvin. I'm so glad he and Mrs. Getty are finally dancing together."

"Speaking of dancing . . ." Alex said.

Marcia hoped he couldn't feel her spine stiffen. She willed her palms to stay dry.

"The West Creek dance?" Alex went on. "Did anybody ask you yet?"

"Not really."

"You want to go to the dance with me?"

"Okay." No, that wasn't strong enough. "Yes," Marcia said. "I want to go to the dance with you."

They kept on dancing. Marcia's heart sang: Thank you, thank you, Agnes Applebaum!

thirteen

Marcia and Sarah both decided to wear glitter eye shadow to the dance. Upstairs in Marcia's bedroom, they sat side by side in front of matching Jay-Dub makeup mirrors, making last-minute adjustments to their hair. In another half hour, the boys would pick them up, chauffeured by Travis's mom.

"Does my hair look greasy?" Sarah asked. "I washed it two hours ago, but it's already getting greasy."

"It looks fine," Marcia told her, staring at her own flushed, excited reflection.

"You didn't even look!"

Marcia obligingly turned and studied Sarah's curly blond hair. Natural blondes had no right ever to complain about anything. "It looks fine."

"Even the bangs? You don't think they're sort of sticking together?"

"No," Marcia reported honestly. Sarah was absolutely, completely, totally beautiful. "Do mine look frizzy? Right around my face?"

"Your hair looks great."

Marcia stood up and faced her full-length mirror sideways, checking for a tummy bulge. In her short, sleeveless black dress, with control-top panty hose underneath, she saw no bulge at all.

"How much weight *have* you lost?" Sarah asked.

"Six pounds," Marcia said. "One hundred ten at the end of August, one hundred four today." She was glad she had lost her tummy bulge. But after so many weeks at West Creek Manor, she no longer thought that a tummy bulge was the most terrible thing in the world.

The phone rang. Marcia ignored it. There was nobody she felt like talking to right now. Alex wasn't the type to call.

Then Marcia's mother pushed open the bedroom door. "It's for you." She held out the phone to Marcia.

Marcia shook her head, irritated at the interruption. "Tell them I'm not here."

"It's one of your teachers," her mother said, sounding concerned. "Ms. Williams."

Marcia slowly accepted the phone. Why on earth would Ms. Williams be calling her at home on a Friday night? She couldn't think of a single thing she had done wrong so far this year, except for letting Madame Cowper see her picture. Ms. Williams couldn't be calling about that. Maybe her mother had heard the name wrong.

"Hello?" Marcia said tentatively.

"Marcia, it's Ms. Williams. I hope I'm not reaching you at a bad time."

It sounded exactly like her. "No," Marcia lied. *It's just the last half hour before my eighth-grade fall dance.*

"I'm afraid I have some sad news."

For a bizarre moment Marcia almost expected Ms. Williams to say that Alex wouldn't be taking her to the dance, after all.

"I just had a call from West Creek Manor. They couldn't remember which of my students was the one doing the beauty makeovers with the residents there. I told them it was you, and they asked me if I'd call you."

Marcia still didn't understand what was happening. Had one of the residents complained about the makeovers? Who could it have been? Everyone loved the makeovers, except for Agnes Applebaum, but Agnes Applebaum wasn't going to say anything against Marcia to one of her teachers.

"Marcia, Mrs. Mavis Getty had a heart attack this afternoon."

"No," Marcia whispered. Ms. Williams couldn't be calling to tell her that Mavis Getty was . . . She couldn't be. She had danced in her wheelchair with Melvin from Nashville just last Saturday at the Oktoberfest.

"She's still alive, but they don't think she'll last the night. She's been asking for you. Well, they think it's you. She keeps talking about 'Diana,' but she also said something about the 'pretty little girl' who did her nails for her."

"She always calls me Diana," Marcia said, her voice breaking.

"She's at West Creek Community Hospital, in intensive care. I don't know whether you'd be willing, or able, to go see her, but . . ."

"I can go. I want to go." She *had* to go.

"This is the first time something like this has happened since I started doing the service learning program with my students. I'm so sorry that it had to happen to you."

Marcia couldn't speak. She was terrified that Mavis Getty might die—and deeply touched that her pitiful little manicures had meant so much to Mrs. Getty at the end of her life.

"I'd better let you go, then," Ms. Williams said. "Thank you, Marcia."

Marcia turned off the phone.

"What happened?" Her mother put her arm around Marcia's shaking shoulders. "Honey, tell me what's wrong."

"I'm not going to the dance." Marcia's voice came out oddly steady, as if someone else, some unrelated stranger, were speaking. "Sarah, tell Alex I can't go. Mom, can you drive me to the hospital? Like, right away? Mavis Getty— she's this friend of mine at the nursing home—well, she's had a heart attack, and Ms. Williams said she's asking for me."

"Tonight?" Marcia's mother sounded incredulous. "You have to go see her *tonight*? It can't wait till tomorrow? Honey, this is your big evening—the dance . . . your dress . . . and you look so pretty . . ."

"They don't think—" The rest of the sentence choked her. She couldn't say it out loud: *They don't think she'll still be here tomorrow.*

Sarah hugged her. Marcia stood there and let Sarah's arms enfold her, and the tears came in a hot torrent.

"Can you drive me now?" she asked her mother when Sarah finally stepped away.

"Do you want to get changed first?"

Marcia shook her head. Mrs. Getty might like to see her little black party dress.

"Well, get your coat, at least." Then her mother gave Marcia a long, hard hug of her own. "I'm proud of you for this."

"Don't let Alex fall in love with anybody else tonight," Marcia told Sarah, trying to force a smile. "No pine nuts!"

"I won't." Sarah's eyes were streaming, too.

"Are you sure you want to do this?" Marcia's mother asked her as they stood together outside the door of Mavis Getty's room in the Intensive Care Unit. "Sometimes it's better to remember people in their healthy state, not spoil your memories by associating them with tubes and things."

Marcia wasn't at all sure she wanted to do this. But she knew she wasn't about to turn back now.

She poked her head into the room. Mavis Getty's large

bulk filled the narrow hospital bed. Mrs. Getty seemed to be asleep. At least, Marcia hoped she was, and not in a coma, or . . . But if you stopped breathing in the ICU, didn't that make bells and sirens go off, and all the nurses come running? No nurses were in the room with her now.

Marcia tiptoed over to the bed. An I.V. tube was taped to Mrs. Getty's left hand, and an oxygen tube ran beneath her nose, but otherwise she looked the same, her face pale and peaceful beneath her red hair, the polish on her fingernails chipped in a couple of places. Heading to the car, Marcia had remembered to grab her Jay-Dub tote bag, just in case.

Was it better to wake her up or let her sleep? Sick people needed their rest, but Marcia couldn't imagine that Mavis Getty would want to sleep through a visitor.

"Mrs. Getty?" she said softly.

Mrs. Getty opened her eyes. "Diana! You did come!" She took a wheezing breath. "I didn't think . . . they'd be able to find you. All I could tell them was . . . Diana, who does my nails."

"What about the real Diana, your great-granddaughter? Is she coming, too?"

"She's in California. They're all in California." Mrs. Getty struggled for another breath. "Well, they're on the plane now. They told me they're coming. But you're . . . you're here right now."

Marcia's throat tightened. She smiled her brightest smile. "Have there been any more developments with . . ."

"With Melvin?" Mrs. Getty tried to laugh, but the laugh turned into a choking cough. Marcia shot a worried look at her mother, still standing silent in the doorway. Then her mother disappeared, probably to find a nurse. Marcia patted Mrs. Getty's hand.

"We went to the chess tournament. Yesterday." Marcia had to lean closer to hear her. "And that man gave me . . . a corsage to wear. Pink carnations. You know how pink clashes . . . with natural red hair. I wore it anyway. Sometimes I'm still amazed"—Marcia could hardly hear her now—"at what men don't know."

"Did he win?"

"Win?"

"The chess tournament?"

Mrs. Getty closed her eyes. Maybe it wasn't good for her to talk so much. But if Mavis Getty had talked through everything in her life except for Elvis Presley on TV, it made sense that she'd talk through a heart attack, too.

Marcia's mother reappeared, with a stern-faced nurse. The nurse bustled over to the bed, checked the placement of the tubes, scanned the monitor by Mrs. Getty's head. It still had lots of squiggles on it, so she had to be alive. Besides, Marcia could hear her breathing, slow and raspy.

"Maybe you should think about going now," the nurse said in a low voice.

"Don't go yet, Diana," Mrs. Getty whispered. Her eyelids fluttered open, and then shut again.

"Is it all right if—well, if I fix her nail polish? A couple of the nails are chipped."

Marcia waited to see if the nurse would say this was the most ridiculous thing she had ever heard in all her years of nursing: to do the nails of an eighty-four-year-old woman who might well be dead in another twenty-four hours.

The nurse's face softened. "Go ahead. Do you have what you need with you?"

Marcia held up her tote bag.

The nurse shook her head, as if bewildered by a girl in a short, slinky, sleeveless black party dress carrying a tote bag full of manicuring supplies to somebody's hospital bed. "Try not to disturb the I.V.," was all she said.

Marcia started to remove the chipped polish from two of Mrs. Getty's right-hand nails. It felt good to be doing some service for Mrs. Getty, however small. Mrs. Getty's fingers felt soft and warm, the way they had always felt. Suddenly Marcia wished she had brought a tape of Elvis Presley for Mrs. Getty to listen to. But Marcia certainly didn't own any Elvis Presley recordings, and her parents didn't, either. Besides, there was nothing in the room for her to play it on.

The nurse stood at the foot of Mrs. Getty's bed, reading the clipboard that had been hanging there.

"Is there any kind of CD player, or tape player, or something?"

"There's one in the nurses' station on the second floor." The nurse's expression was guarded, her tone noncommittal. Maybe she thought Marcia wanted to blare rock music all through Intensive Care.

"Mrs. Getty was—is—a big fan of Elvis Presley, and I thought she might like to hear"—Marcia tried to remember the song that Mavis Getty had sung into Lizzie's tape recorder on the day they had met—" 'Love Me Tender.' "

"And you happen to have a collection of Elvis Presley tapes in your tote bag, too?" The nurse was smiling now.

"No, but— Mom? The mall isn't far from here, and the stores are still open . . ."

Marcia's mother stood up from her chair by the door. She, too, looked relieved at having something to do. "You'll be all right by yourself?"

"I'll be all right."

Half an hour later, Mrs. Getty's nails were drying, the CD player from the second-floor nurses' station was plugged in beside the bed, and a CD of Elvis's greatest hits was ready to play.

"Mrs. Getty?" Mrs. Getty didn't open her eyes, but her grip on Marcia's hand tightened. "I have a surprise for you."

Marcia signaled to her mother to press the PLAY button on the CD player. "Love me tender," Elvis crooned into the quiet room.

Mrs. Getty's eyes flew open. "Diana. You're still here," she whispered to Marcia. "I thought I had died and gone to heaven."

Mrs. Getty drifted back to sleep as Marcia held her freshly manicured hand, and Elvis Presley kept on singing.

fourteen

Mr. Morrison stood next to Marcia's desk a week later, gazing down at the four portraits she had brought in to show him: Mavis Getty, Mabel Thompson, Alberta Estes, and Agnes Applebaum. Marcia wasn't afraid of what he would say this time. She knew the pictures were good. Not as good as she wanted them to be, not as good as Rembrandt's, but so much better than her quick sketch of Madame Cowper. Her work had come such a long way.

Mr. Morrison was silent. Maybe he *didn't* like them, after all? Maybe he was trying to find the right sarcastic remark?

"It's wonderful, isn't it," he finally said, "what you can do when you learn to look with your eyes *and* your heart. We'll hang these in the fall show."

Marcia felt herself flushing with proud pleasure at his praise. It was a major honor to have your work included in the fall art show. And Mr. Morrison definitely wasn't the type who displayed work he didn't respect just to make a student feel good.

He turned to go to the next desk. Marcia somehow

couldn't bear for him to walk away not even knowing about Mrs. Getty.

"Mr. Morrison?"

He turned back.

"This lady here? She died. Last weekend. She was all excited about this big party at the nursing home, and she had gotten a new boyfriend, and everything, and then she had a heart attack, and died."

It was clear that Mr. Morrison didn't know what Marcia expected him to say. "I'm sorry. Would you rather not display this portrait in the show?"

"No, it's just that—I never knew anybody who died before. And she was the most alive of anybody there."

"And she's still alive here," Mr. Morrison said. "This is why artists need to speak the truth, while they can."

The art show was part of the West Creek Middle School fall open house. The featured art hung in the hallways for parents to admire as they stopped by various classrooms and chatted with their children's teachers. Marcia's pictures had been placed outside Madame Cowper's room. Marcia hoped Madame Cowper wouldn't see them and remember her other drawing. But Madame Cowper was probably too busy showing off her students' French compositions to spend time loitering in the hall.

Marcia let her parents wander on their own from classroom to classroom while she stood guard by her pictures with Gwennie. "Why am I standing here like a dope?" she asked Gwennie.

"Because you're proud of your work, and you should be."

"What if someone doesn't know they're mine and says something bad about them?"

"They won't, and if they did, it would say more about them than about you. Come on, Marsh, your teacher wouldn't display them if he didn't think they were good."

Marcia had a sweet, bragging thought that she wouldn't have shared even with Gwennie: her teacher wouldn't display them if he didn't think they were *outstandingly* good.

Lizzie and her mother stopped by first. Lizzie pulled her mother to a halt in front of the pictures, and they both stared at them in unmistakably appreciative silence.

When Lizzie looked away, she had tears in her eyes. "They're beautiful," she whispered. "All four of them. Four completely different, completely beautiful women. I can't believe . . ." She gently touched Mavis Getty's broad, smiling face, her bright red hair. "I can't believe she's gone. But I look at this picture, and she *isn't* gone."

Lizzie's mother gave Marcia a quick hug. "You're a very talented artist, Marcia. There's nothing harder than a portrait, in my view. Anyone can draw an apple. An apple doesn't have a soul."

Marcia remembered her struggle to draw an apple that didn't look like a red tennis ball.

"Apples have souls!" she and Lizzie both said together.

Mrs. Archer laughed. "I stand corrected. When the great artists paint an apple, they make us believe that it *does* have a soul. But I still insist that portraits are more challenging. And these are especially fine ones."

"Would you let us publish these in the literary magazine?" Lizzie asked. "I'd understand if you think they're too private to be published, but they're so beautiful. They'd be the best thing in the magazine."

Marcia looked at Gwennie. "Sure," she said. Mavis Getty would get to be a "pinup girl" in a school magazine, after all.

As Lizzie and her mother wandered off, Sarah and Travis ambled down the hall, his arm draped over her shoulders, too focused on each other to pay any attention to the world of art. Marcia still felt a pang of jealousy at the sight of them. She and Alex had talked a few times since the dance, enough for her to know he wasn't mad at her for standing him up, but not enough to bring back the moment they had shared at the Oktoberfest.

Then Alex himself appeared, with Dave, Ethan, and Julius. The boys stopped to check out the pictures. Marcia wondered if Alex would make a wisecrack. "Look at those old bags," was the kind of thing Alex might say. But he had spent time at West Creek Manor, too.

"Wow," Ethan said.

"I didn't know you could draw like that," Julius said.

Dave struck the pose of *The Thinker*, fist to chin. "Draw me!"

Alex shoved him. "Yeah, you could call it *Portrait of a Jerk*," he jeered good-naturedly. Dave shoved him back.

The other boys drifted on. Alex remained behind. Gwennie shot Marcia a meaningful look and obligingly disappeared.

"How's it going?" Alex asked her. "That has to be rough—having someone you know die like that."

Marcia felt tears stinging her eyes. Alex reached out and took her hand. For a moment they stood there together, in front of the portraits, hand in hand, without speaking.

Then: "Saturday," he said.

"Saturday?"

"The day of reckoning. The day of leaf raking. The day on which I rake the leaves of the Faitak family's famous tree. I was hoping we'd get one of West Creek's eighty-mile-an-hour winds and all the leaves would blow away. But my mom says I can't put it off any longer. So—one o'clock? Will you be there?"

"I'll be there."

Alex finally let go of Marcia's hand when Ms. Williams descended upon them.

"I've always been committed to service learning as a wonderful way of teaching social studies," she said, "but now I can also claim that it's a wonderful way of teaching art." Ms. Williams wasn't the hugging type, but she put her arm around Marcia and gave her shoulder a small squeeze before she went on her way.

Alex left to catch up with his friends. Old Mr. Adams poked his head out of the math room.

"Miss Faitak," he greeted her, in the stiff, formal way he had.

Marcia gave him a friendly wave. "Come see my pictures!" It was time to launch her dating service for the elderly. She had decided against introducing Melvin-from-Nashville to Alberta Estes. He belonged to Mavis Getty forever. But Mr. Adams was definitely a possibility.

"First-rate, Miss Faitak!" Mr. Adams waggled his thick white eyebrows at her.

"This one's my favorite." Marcia pointed to the portrait of Alberta Estes. "I couldn't make her as beautiful as she is in real life, but I tried. She's beautiful on the inside, too, so sweet and kind. Oh, and she's good at math. She was a whiz at math when she was in school."

Was Marcia imagining it, or was Mr. Adams studying Alberta's portrait with special interest?

"You're . . . single, aren't you, Mr. Adams?"

He gave a wheezing laugh. "Miss Faitak, are you matchmaking?"

Marcia gave him a wide-eyed, innocent smile. He headed on down the hall. Well, a seed had been planted, at least.

Madame Cowper came out into the hall now, too. Traffic inside the classrooms was thinning. Marcia felt torn between two impulses: to position herself so that she would block Madame Cowper's view of her pictures, and to turn tail and run away. Instead, she tried the same wide-eyed, innocent smile that she had used on Mr. Adams, the smile that said, All right, you've caught me in the act, but I'm covering as best I can. From years of practice on her parents, Marcia had found it was a smile that worked better on men than on women. Unfortunately, Madame Cowper was not a man.

"*Qu'est-ce que nous avons ici?* What have we here? Are these your pictures?"

Marcia nodded. Madame Cowper stepped forward to examine them more closely. "*Magnifique!*" she exclaimed. "These old women, you love them very much, *oui*?"

Marcia nodded again.

"We can tell," Madame Cowper said. "The love shines through."

It was time for Marcia to speak. "I had to learn how to do that. At first—I didn't know." Would Madame Cowper understand what she was trying to say?

Madame Cowper gave one of her low, rich chuckles. "You knew how to draw the double chin, eh? But not yet the spirit within." She was looking at the portrait of Mavis Getty as she spoke, but Marcia knew that Madame Cowper was remembering the other picture, and forgiving her for not knowing then what she knew now.

"The French have a wonderful term for an older woman," Madame Cowper said. "*Une femme d'un certain âge*. A woman of a certain age. A woman whose age we do not name. A woman who is ageless."

Marcia's parents reappeared, with Gwennie.

"Your daughter, she is a very talented girl," Madame Cowper told them.

Marcia's dad beamed. "No doubt about it, I've got two of the most wonderful girls in the world." He slipped one arm around Marcia and the other around Gwennie and gave them both a squeezing hug.

"*Bonsoir,*" Madame Cowper said. "Good night."

Madame Cowper slipped back inside her classroom.

"Ready to head out?" Marcia's dad asked her.

Marcia nodded. She followed her family down the hall, after one silent, backward glance at the portrait of Mavis Getty.

It was cold on Saturday, the sky low and gray, snow forecast by evening. Marcia hoped the frigid breeze wouldn't make her nose too red for Alex. Red cheeks were one thing, but a red nose was another, and a red and dripping nose was worst of all. She zipped herself into her favorite, straight-legged jeans, relieved that they fit her once again, and laid out the blue hat and scarf that matched her eyes.

Promptly at one o'clock, Alex presented himself at Marcia's door. Her father answered the bell.

"So you're ready to do some raking," he said jovially. "Well, do we have leaves for you!"

Marcia saw that Alex had brought his own rake. His head was uncovered, but he had on a warm jacket and sturdy work gloves. He grinned at her dad. "I'm ready, sir."

"Start by getting them raked into one big pile. Then Marcia here can help you with the bagging."

"I can help him with the raking, too," Marcia said.

"How did I end up such a lucky man?" Marcia's father asked. "Everyone seems to want to rake my leaves."

Marcia was grateful that he left them alone once they were outside.

"You don't have to do this, you know," Alex said when Marcia started awkwardly dragging her rake through the thick carpet of leaves. "I'm the one who T.P.ed the tree, not you."

But I'm glad you did it. I even saved a scrap of the toilet paper in my treasure box. "Well, it's good exercise," Marcia said.

"Yeah, so is breaking rocks in a quarry."

They raked for a while in silence. Alex was better at raking than Marcia and covered twice as much ground in the same amount of time, though Marcia could have raked more if she hadn't been watching Alex to see if he was watching her. He wasn't. When Alex had a job to do, apparently he *did* it.

Marcia was getting tired. She felt a blister forming on her right hand, between her thumb and forefinger.

"Had enough?" Alex asked her.

"I just need a little rest." She laid her rake down on the lawn.

"It seems a shame," Alex remarked conversationally, "to have such a huge, deep pile of leaves, and nobody to throw into it."

Marcia's heart soared. "You wouldn't dare!"

In answer, Alex dropped his own rake and grabbed hold of Marcia's arms. In one swift motion, he had her in the leaf pile, half buried in leaves, her hat knocked off, bits of broken leaves in her hair.

"Alex, I'll get you for this!"

Marcia struggled up, lunged at Alex, and tried to shove him into the leaf pile. They both tumbled into the dry, warm, sweet-smelling leaves together, Alex's arms around her, her arms around him.

I'll have to save a leaf in the box with the toilet paper! Marcia thought. *Wait till I tell Agnes Applebaum!*